The Ghosts of Rose Hill

For Jacob and Miriam,
who led me out of the woods
—R. M. R.

Published by
Peachtree Teen
An imprint of PEACHTREE PUBLISHING COMPANY INC.
1700 Chattahoochee Avenue
Atlanta, Georgia 30318-2112
PeachtreeBooks.com

Edited by Ashley Hearn
Design and composition by Adela Pons
Cover design by Isabel Ibañez

Printed and bound in May 2022 at Thomson Reuters, Eagan, MN, USA.
10 9 8 7 6 5 4 3 2

ISBN: 978-1-68263-338-0

Cataloging-in-Publication Data is available from the Library of Congress.

R. M. ROMERO

The Ghosts of Rose Hill

PEACHTREE
Teen

"She made herself stronger by fighting with the wind."

—Frances Hodgson Burnett

First Movement:
The Golden City

Chapter One

The city I was born in
embraces each person
who steps off the mainland
and onto the island
known as Miami Beach.
It understands
we have nowhere else to go.

A dozen countries
converge here;
languages tangle
like bright ribbons
in the humid air.

Nearly everyone
on the island is an expat,

a survivor of a tragedy
that swallowed their family
and nation
whole.

So the last thing I expected
was to be exiled
by my own parents.

When my grades
in math and science
slipped
last semester,
when my PSAT score
was less than ideal,
my parents blamed:

> my best friends,
> Sarah and Martina,
> the parties
> I sometimes went to,
> my obsession
> with playing the violin.

They even asked
if I was sneaking around
with a boy.
I swore I wasn't;
they didn't believe me.

Dad scowled
as he looked over
my report card;
Mom raised her voice
like a fist
as she lectured me.

I almost named you Marisol,
because the sea gave me freedom—
the freedom to do
and say whatever I like.
I studied hard;
la pluma no pesa—
the pen has no weight.
You must do the same.
Do not waste
what the sea and I
have given you!

I'm glad
she didn't name me
after the ocean—
it's much too powerful.
I'm just a girl
who dreams about magic
and can't wrap her mind
around algebraic equations.

Chapter Two

My mother's family,
Lopez,
came from Cuba.

Lopez means:
son of Lope,
son of wolf.

But it's the Lopez *women*
who have always howled the loudest.
They had to be fierce
and stubborn
to survive.

My great-grandmothers
      (may their memories
      be a blessing)
mastered the art of escape
seven generations
before my mother.

They fled the pyres
      (the flames
      fueled by hatred)
devouring

the street corners,
synagogues,
cemeteries
of Spain,
crossing the ocean
with their faith
and Shabbat candlesticks
tucked under their skirts.

I wonder
if they understood
their ancestors would leave Cuba
      with its sunset-colored buildings
      and blue skies as soft as whispers
the same way.

When Castro
      (and his communists)
rose to power,
he waved his cigar like a magic wand.
Whenever he did,
poets and gossips,
friends and neighbors
disappeared,
taken by men who prowled
through the night.

Mom understood

what happened to those who vanished,
how their bones were planted
in fields of rice
and sugarcane.

Not wanting to be among them
      (and knowing one day
       she might be)
Mom fled her island,
letting the water carry her
and her little fishing boat
away to a new life
with nothing
but the dress she wore to her name.

Like a queen of Narnia
who couldn't go back
through the wardrobe,
Mom knows
she'll never return to Cuba again.

She'll be in exile
forever.

My parents decide
they'll be sending me to live
with my aunt Žofie
in Prague

the golden city
of a hundred towers
and a thousand stories
for the summer.

They think
if I'm away from Miami
        (and all its distractions)
I'll study more seriously
for the college admissions exams
looming
in my future.

The bargain is this:
in the fall,
I must earn 1300
        (or above)
on the SAT.
Mom and Dad
see that score as a silver key;
it will grant me access
to the best colleges,
the largest scholarships,
the brightest future.

But if my score is any lower,
there will be
        no more music lessons

or weekend outings
until it improves.

At first,
my father raged
like a September storm
at the idea of banishing me
to the city
he grew up in.

He told my mother:
Žofie lives her life
on top of bones!
The communists are gone,
but what they did with
> *their tanks,*
> *their lies and laws,*
> *their secret police*
can't be erased.
I haven't been back
in almost thirty years.
I'll never go back again.

Mom said: *You and I*
didn't survive
dictators of flesh and blood
so we could live
in fear of ghosts.

And you're lucky—
your daughter can visit
the place you were born
and be safe.

She won the argument
by virtue of being right.
          (She usually does.)

June, July, and August
lie ahead,
three months
without my friends
or my violin.
I'm being separated
from everyone,
everything,
supposedly leading me
down
the wrong path
in life.

I tell myself:
my friendships will survive
a single summer away.
Sarah, Martina, and I
can still talk
every day.

But how will I live
without
my music?

Chapter Three

The night before I leave,
I meet Sarah and Martina
at the bus stop to say goodbye.

Their parents send them
to the New World School of the Arts,
where they study
cello, opera,
how to transform
strings of notes on a page
into tales about:
swan girls,
queens of night,
and wolves
with wild intentions.

I begged
Mom and Dad to let me attend
the same high school.
I wanted nothing more

than to study music,
play violin,
be with my friends.

But they refused.

Music,
my parents said,
won't put food on the table.
Music,
they said,
won't give me the kind of life
they so desperately want
for me.

They believe
we can hold
safety and security
in our hands,
building it
       one degree,
       one car,
       one house
at a time.
Only when our roots are stone
will we be safe.

My friends and I
flee the packs of tourists
drinking up the neon glow
of Ocean Drive
and race down to the beach.

But by the time
we reach the water,
I'm already
                              outside
their conversation.

Sarah and Martina
will spend their sixteenth summers
here in Miami Beach,
chasing songs and kisses,
making memories
steeped in wondrous colors.
But I won't share
any of their adventures.
I'll only see them captured
in pictures and videos,
with an ocean between us.

I wade into the waves
as my friends chatter away.
All I can do
is float—

I've been left behind
by them.
     (Again.)

For as long as I can remember,
I've written letters in sea foam
to the mermaids
I once believed
swam just off the shore.

For years, I asked them:
     Do you hide when the hurricanes come?
     Do you pray to the tides?
     Do you fight sharks with your teeth and tridents?
     What's it like, to be you?

They never answered.
Mermaids
are terrible correspondents.

Still, I let my words
     drip
          down
my fingers,
bitter with salt.

My final letter, before departure:
Did the sea ever swallow up your songs?
Have you ever let
a human boy
pluck them off your tongue
and carry them up to the sun?
Did your mother or father
ever take your music away,
like my parents took mine?

> *PS*
> *I know I can always count*
> *on your silence.*
> *It's my own*
> *I'm not used to.*

Being trapped
inside an airplane
      (thirteen hours to Prague,
      with one transfer in London)
allows me to sink into
Tallis Fantasia
      (Vaughan Williams, 1910)
on my headphones.
I ignore the exam workbooks
I should be reading;
the curtain of stars

we soar through
captures my attention entirely.

If only I could keep flying
and never
touch the ground
again.

Chapter Four

Aunt Žofie comes to find me
in the gray airport terminal.
I barely recognize her;
we've only met
in person
once before.

> (But her two-week visit to Miami
> contained a lifetime's worth of arguments
> with my father.)

You'll enjoy your summer here,
Aunt Žofie promises me,
slinging my bag
over her shoulder
as if it's no heavier
than a dust mote.

I know my brother
expects you to do nothing
but study.
He didn't want you to come
in the first place.

But Prague is a place
where a girl your age
can find herself.
I'll let you have your freedom,
as long
as you're careful.
We're very much alike,
you and I.

I doubt that.
Aunt Žofie is a storm
who only pretends to be a woman.
Her hair drifts above her head,
a cloud of thoughts
and enchantments.

And according to my parents,
I'm a doctor, lawyer, engineer, architect
in waiting,
one who hasn't quite grown
into a practical future
without music.

(Or mermaids.)
(Or magic.)

Aunt Žofie calls her house Růžová Chata:
Rose Cottage.
It sits on Růžová Kopec:
Rose Hill.
But if you looked on a map,
you wouldn't find either of them.

She speaks
Czech
and English,
Russian
and German.

But sometimes
I can't understand
a single word
she says.
Her heart's language is a mystery
I can't solve.

There's no order
to Rose Cottage's four rooms,
which makes it the opposite
of my own home.

The walls
are pitted and cracked.
My aunt's chairs bleed stuffing
when I sit on them.
Her computer is a relic,
built before I was born.
Jars of paint compete for space
with crumpled sketches,
oceans of dust,
and books fattened by poetry.

As I stare,
Aunt Žofie tells me:
My home
may not look like much,
but I have everything I need!
I can visit museums
whenever I like.
I can walk to the library
where the walls are painted
with the stars
of a hundred constellations
and every book
invites me inside.

I wonder
if the real reason
my parents sent me here

is to see how humble
the life of an artist is.

My father's and Aunt Žofie's stories
diverged
when they were only a little older
than I am.

Dad became a scientist in America.
His world is made up of:

        atoms,

        particles,

        waves.

Aunt Žofie became an artist in Prague.
She makes her *own* world filled with:

        faeries,

        river spirits,

        and queens.

Maybe brothers and sisters
must always contradict each other
so that the world
stays in balance.

I wouldn't know anything
about siblings.
I have no brothers;

my only sisters are the friends
I won't see
until September.

And Martina and Sarah
haven't reached out
since we left the beach
and they started their own adventure
                    together.

Without me.

Chapter Five

The sun pulls me from my bed
my second morning in Prague.
I follow the light
into Aunt Žofie's garden,
where hundreds of roses bloom.
They come in shades
of cotton-candy pink
and vivid red,
like kisses.

I climb the hill
behind the cottage,

a prayer
drifting
through my head.
>   *(We praise You,*
>   *Eternal God,*
>   *Sovereign*
>   *of the universe,*
>   *who creates fragrant flowers*
>   *and herbs.)*

By the time I reach the top of the hill
>   (Rose Hill)

the backs of my legs
burn like the sunrise
splashed across the sky.

From here, I can see:
the blue walls of Rose Cottage,
a dark snake of concrete road,
the black towers of Prague Castle,
the arch of Charles Bridge
spanning the Vltava River,
which flows all the way to Austria.

I fling my arms out,
trying to gather the city
in my hands.

Behind me is a grove of trees.
The alders and ash
devour
the pink light of dawn;
the wind
makes them laugh and shiver.

I venture into the little wood.
Any secret I bury
between these trees
would never find its way out.

In the gloom of the forest,
an old stone rises
from the ground.
A lion is carved on its rough face,
his mouth open
in a silent roar.
Ropes of ivy and moss
crawl
up his sides,
the green cloak of a once
and future king.

What are you?
Who put you all the way up here?
I ask the great cat.

The lion must know
what my history books forgot,
but time
has swallowed his voice.
He doesn't answer;
he can't.

The greenery
ensnaring the stone is an invader;
it conquered Rose Hill
long before I was born.
But I want to see the lion
in all his glory.

I struggle,
trying
to pull the vines away.
As I move, my ankle
bumps
against something solid.

It's another stone,
this one made of white marble.
I shift
lost October leaves from its base,
exposing letters
I've been learning
since I was a child.

Yud.
Ayin.
Aleph.

Hebrew.

I whisper:
You were Jewish.
Like Mom.
Like me.

There aren't many Jews left in Prague;
the Shoah
        (the greatest shipwreck
        of our People)
stole them away,
leaving their books,
their songs,
their stories behind.

But the Jews of Prague
are all around me here.
Their dust grows up
through the earth;
their hands reach for me.

This is a *cemetery*,
I realize.

And I don't think anyone remembers
it's here.

Anyone
       except
             for
                  me.

I feel eyes moving over me
as I trace
the letters on the headstone—
the *matzevah.*
I stumble back,
asking the alders:
Hello? Ahoj?

The woods
refuse to speak.
But I'm not alone.

There is a boy
standing between the trees.
His eyes are the blue of the sea
I left behind.
He's taller than me
and slim as a birch rod
with soft dark curls
I want to wrap my fingers around.
We must be the same age.

My voice is more certain now.
My name is Ilana.
Do you live nearby?
Do you know my aunt Žofie?

The boy pulls back
like the tide.
Now I wish
I hadn't shouted.
I take a step forward,
but the boy is gone
in a flicker of my lashes,
leaving the shadows
settling like crows
in the space
where he stood.

I saw a boy,
on top of Rose Hill,
I tell Aunt Žofie
when I return to the cottage.
My heart has crawled up my throat;
I'm so excited
I can barely breathe around it.

Did he have blue eyes?
My aunt
holds a chipped teacup

between two fingers,
like it, too, is one of her many
paintbrushes.

> (I can tell her mind is only
> half
> with me.
> The rest of her is a permanent resident
> of Fairyland,
> where the borders are closed
> to nearly everyone.)

When I nod, Aunt Žofie says:
I've seen him too.
He used to live near here, I think.
Although he hasn't lived anywhere
for a long time.
I'm surprised he let you see him at all.
Having a ghost
is like having a cat.
They wander where they like
and won't come
when you call.

A ghost?
The word sparks
on my tongue.
That makes sense—

there's a Jewish cemetery
at the top of Rose Hill.
Did you know that?

There's a story
printed
in Aunt Žofie's gaze,
but it's in a language
I haven't learned to read.
      (Yet.)
I knew the stones there
held some meaning.
But I've always preferred
not to climb the hill myself.
I don't care for ghosts.

Could I clean the cemetery a little?
Trim back the trees,
make the matzevot *visible again?*
I hold my breath,
expecting to be exiled
from the graveyard
as I was exiled from Miami.

Aunt Žofie sets her cup down.
I'm not Jewish—you are.
That gives you a connection
to the cemetery

that I'll never have.
You should do
whatever you think is right.
But wear gloves
and be careful, Ilana.
Keep your head down
as you work.
Don't talk to the ghost boy
again.

I can't help but ask:
Why not?

Aunt Žofie
squeezes my hand.
I appreciate Prague's magic.
I paint it
each and every day.
But not all magic is safe,
and there are things here
far worse
than ghosts.
By speaking to the dead,
you might draw them to you.

Let the boy on the hill go;
let him move on.
You don't belong in his world

and he has stopped belonging
in ours.

The boy and his death
don't unsettle me,
regardless of what Aunt Žofie says.

Most of the stories
Mom and Dad tell me
are ghost stories.

So why wouldn't I want
to talk to the dead?

If I were in Miami, I'd know
what to do
for the boy on Rose Hill.

I'd know
whether he'd want me
to find ten men
and say Kaddish.

I'd know
if I should offer a prayer
to the Orishas—
Yemoya,
Oko,

Osanyin,
    (who live
    in the water
    and the soil)
on his behalf.

I'd know
if I should feed him
bread and sugar,
as if his soul
were a hummingbird,
swift and bright.

But I don't know anything
about the boy in Prague,
except the color of his eyes.

Tomorrow morning
when the world is cool and misty,
I'll climb the hill
and tend to the *matzevot*.
The dead boy's name
must be engraved on one of them.

I want to know it;
then it can be a blessing.
Then I can remember him
the right way.

Chapter Six

Aunt Žofie needs art supplies;
I need gardening gloves
to fight
the cemetery's stinging nettles.
We leave Rose Cottage
and walk toward the city center
in search of both.

My aunt tells me about Prague
as we cross Charles Bridge,
watched by the statues of saints
       (black with coal dust and age)
neither of us
put our faith in.

Prague's always confusing itself.
It doesn't know
what's part of its true history
and what is a story
people tell about it.

It can't remember
if it was built by travelers
or a woman named Libuše

who could see the future,
if Rabbi Loew was a scholar
or a magician
who made a soldier
out of clay
to protect
the Jewish people here.

It doesn't know
if the birch groves are silent
or if they're full of vila—
enchanted women
whose beauty
haunts
the minds of foresters.

Prague believes in magic.
Prague believes in itself.

(I wish
I could be more like Prague.)

Dad never tells stories like Aunt Žofie's
when he mentions Prague.
Every word that leaves his mouth
about the city
is newsprint gray.

When I was younger, he said:
The communist government
demanded
we all believe
the same things,
cultivate
the same dreams.
If we defied them,
they stole our voices
and what little freedom
we had.

I wanted a future
I couldn't have in Prague.
I wanted more than breadlines
and secrets.
So I ran,
trying to make myself
into a ghost, unseen and unheard,
as I walked to freedom
through Austria.
Then I came here, to America.
A refugee.

I nodded along
with this sad tale.
If I closed my eyes,
I thought I could feel

the echo of Dad's journey
out of Prague
in my own bones.

Maybe
my father is still running from Prague.
Maybe
my mother is still fleeing Havana.
Maybe
my entire family is still trying to escape history.

(But if that's true,
what am I doing here,
drowning in it?)

The buildings that block out
the morning sun
in the city center
are older than any in America.

Bullet holes are visible
on the doorways,
old wounds
in need of healing.
Bottles of absinthe glow,
green as Rose Hill's forest,
in dusty shop windows.
Posters in gleeful electric colors

promise dance clubs
full of beautiful boys,
glittering girls,
music guaranteed
to set a person's soul alight.

Martina and Sarah finally write back
after I send them photos
of all the forbidden things
at my fingertips.
For the first time,
they're jealous of *me*.

But I don't want to chase
the green fairy
or lose myself
in the arms of a stranger
after dark.

There's only one thing
I want now.
And no one
        (not even Prague itself)
can give me a lifetime of music.

The earthy smell of Turkish coffee
welcomes us inside a café
hidden away

between the houses and museums
where the centuries
blur together.

The walls are whipped-cream white;
the tiles lemon custard yellow.
Even our chairs are licorice red,
weeping
cotton-candy wisps of stuffing.

All the other patrons
sketch, write poetry,
tap out rhythms
on the edges of tables
as they sip their coffee.
Prague is old,
but her streets are dancing.

Aunt Žofie says:
This city's become popular
with Westerners
who weren't allowed here
before the old government
changed hands
with the new.
They think they can become
the next Picasso
if they let Prague into their hearts.

Even if the artists fail,
I still envy them;
I haven't created
anything
in what feels like forever.

I am just a tangled mess of notes
that don't make up a song
and barely
make up a girl.

No one looks up
when Aunt Žofie orders us coffee,
her voice thunderclap loud.
They're too lost
in the worlds they're making
to pay attention
to what's happening
in this one.

My brother told me
you want to be a musician, says Aunt Žofie.
He also told me
it wasn't practical—
as if being practical
ever matters
when it comes to art.

I shrug.
He's right.
I can't make money
playing the violin.
It won't give me
stability in life.

You've seen Rose Cottage—
it's a simple place, Aunt Žofie replies.
But I earn enough
with my paintings
to keep coffee in my cup
and a roof
over my head.
And when I need to see the sky
open like a book,
I take the train out of the city.
What more do I need?

Aunt Žofie soon leaves her coffee
           (and me)
behind
to greet another artist,
his fingers smudged with paint.

I'm relieved.
Now I don't have to disappoint her
with the truth:

I can't defy my parents,
I can't be like her.

I do what I'm told.

Outside,
a little girl is staring into the café,
pressing her pale hands
against the window.

Her dress
is the color of strawberries,
her dark eyes are filled with wishes
for sour cherry jam
and squares of milk chocolate—
everything
just out of her reach.

I wave, but the girl
only scowls at me.
The rose
       (the petals
       the pale yellow of old
       forgotten lace)
tucked behind her ear
flutters
each time she moves.

It looks
as if it's sprouted
from her very skin.

I close my eyes
against the sight of her
and the impossibility of her flower.
Today
has been strange enough
already.

When Aunt Žofie returns,
the strawberry girl is gone,
taking the wonders
     (caught like pebbles)
in the soles of her shoes
with her.

Chapter Seven

My aunt and I go from shop to shop,
the sun striking my back
like a fist.
We follow her list of items,
a trail of bread crumbs
that will

     (eventually)
take us home.

Aunt Žofie purchases:
tubes of paint,
new brushes,
reels of canvas so large
they could cover Prague's streets.
I buy:
leather gloves,
thick socks,
a sun hat—
protection
against the forest
trying to overtake the cemetery.

Every shop we visit is hidden away,
the rooms so cold
December itself
would feel at home in them.
I wasn't built for places like this;
July blazes in my blood.
I ask to wait outside
before I freeze.

I dance to keep warm,
so that my skin remembers
summer hasn't ended yet.

I still have time to change
my future—
whatever it may be.

I don't wander the streets
in my aunt's absence,
but my gaze does,
traveling
up, up, up
over the rooftops
before coming to rest
on the house across the way.

The building looks like a rotten tooth,
black and chipped.
A hundred years of dust
have turned the windows silver.
Anything
could be hidden
beneath that glaze.

A man in a butter-yellow suit
perches like a falcon
on the front steps.
His tie bounces
in time with the music
he summons
from the black violin

propped beneath his chin.
The instrument's silver strings
steal the sunlight.

The man smiles
as he plays.
His front teeth are crooked,
fence posts bent in the wind.
The notes of his song
slide
through the gap
between them.

He looks happier
than anyone
I've seen in Prague so far.

The music
drags me
across the cobblestones,
demanding
I go forward.

In Miami,
there are riptides
that will pull you under the water,
        leaving you
                beneath the waves

with no mermaids to raise you up
from the depths.

This feels
like a riptide,
drawing me out
from the shore.

But where
is it
taking
me?

Up close,
the man with the violin
is younger than Aunt Žofie
or any of the adults in my life.
But he is still more grown-up
than I am.

His black hair is faded,
like someone's memory
of a night sky.
But there are no stars
in this man's eyes.
One is hazel;
the other is white
as a cup of milk.

The stranger asks:
Mohu vám pomoci?
Can I help you?
His German accent
wraps around
each Czech
and English word
like a wool scarf.

"Un bel dì, vedremo" from Madame Butterfly, I say.
That's what you were playing,
wasn't it?

The man's face lights up,
bright as the summer sun.
You're a musician then!
Wonderful!
My name is Rudolf Wassermann.
And you are ...?

I fumble for a name
that isn't mine
> (never give your real name
> to a stranger;
> they could be
> the wrong sort of angel
> and gobble it up)

but I can never be anyone else
except me.
I'm Ilana.

Wassermann laughs,
bouncing
up
on his toes.
It's wonderful to meet you, Ilana!
Do you play the violin?
You must!

I step away from Wassermann.
But the cobblestones
catch at my heels,
trying to shove me back to him.
I used to.
But not anymore.
I left my violin somewhere else.

Wassermann taps his chin
in time
with the music
that must be buzzing
in his veins.
Well then,
someone will just have to find you
a new violin.

A person should never be
without their music
for too long.

He spreads his hands,
white as the pages of a book
I haven't read yet.
I follow the gesture down
and see the truth,
an absence
written on the cobblestones
too firmly for me to deny.

Wassermann
has no shadow.

I look up,
but he is already gone,
just like the boy
on Rose Hill.

Chapter Eight

I rise with the sun
the following morning, unable
to sleep any longer.

My mind knows
I'm in Prague,
but my body insists
I haven't left Miami.
I've traveled,
not only across space
but through time.

I pull out my workbooks,
but soon, I stray
from the diagrams,
the strings of vocabulary words
better left
in the mouths of poets.

Aunt Žofie told me
she must paint by moonlight;
I must use the sunlight
to peel away the mysteries
from Rose Hill's cemetery.

> (I can study
> anytime.
> Can't I?)

I dig
through the garden shed,
retrieve

hedge trimmers,
gloves,
my sense of determination.

Flower petals
cling to my tools;
I shake them off as I climb the hill.
Tomorrow,
the edges of the petals
will crumble
and brown,
like strawberry girl's roses.

But today,
they are ballerinas
in summertime skirts
who dance only for me.

The dead boy
isn't in the graveyard now.
But maybe
if I'm quiet,
he'll show himself again.

What to wear
in a haunted cemetery:

A pair of jeans
as soft and pale as sand,
my new sun hat,
its brim half as wide as the river,
burns from nettles
that wrap around my ankles
like bracelets,
blisters that sting
whenever I flex my hands,
secrets
up against my skin.

Things I'm forbidden to do
in a Jewish cemetery:

Disturb the bones.
The dead are resting, waiting
to be called back to life.

(Or so the Torah tells us.)

Bring any of the following—
a kohen,
a Torah scroll,
food,
cigarettes,
mourners after nightfall.

This is what I should do:
honor the dead, always.

I don't know where to put
the saplings
and branches
I cut away.
I drag them halfway down Rose Hill.
An hour later,
it looks like I've moved
an entire forest.

Calluses build up like empires
across my palms.
But I feel the way I used to
when I strung the right notes together
on my violin,
as if what I'm doing *matters*.

I never knew
the people buried here
in life.
But if I don't take care of this place,
who *will*?

Chapter Nine

The ghost boy
weaves between the trees,
appearing in patches of sunlight
like a stray cat.

I keep my head down,
trying
not to meet
his ocean-blessed eyes.

I can see the woods through him,
gray and shimmering,
as if the trees are ghosts too.
His hair runs like ink,
like all the things
he hasn't said to me.
      (But might.)

You can see me.
The boy's voice
is a spring breeze,
lost
in the sticky heat of summer.
I'm surprised
he speaks English,

but maybe I shouldn't be.
Who's to say
the living
and the dead
can't learn from each other?

I can see you.
I sit back on my haunches,
careful
not to make
the dry leaves rustle.
Too much noise
is bound to scare him away.

The boy is the only person my age
I've talked to
since I left Miami.
I didn't realize
how much I missed it
until now.

I'm Ilana.
What's your name?

I'm.
I'm Benjamin.
The boy's fingers twitch
at his sides,

like he wants to take my hand,
but has fallen
out of practice.
It must be hard
to recall how to be alive
when you've been mist and memory
for years.

A rose
blooms from his collar.
I want to think
the color of Benjamin's petals
     (lavender,
        like first light)
is hopeful.
They are more vivid
than the flower worn
     (or grown)
by the little girl
at the café.

I don't mean to be rude,
but why are you here?
Benjamin asks.
Why do you care
about this cemetery?

I pluck my gloves off,
finger by finger.

The dirt caked in the leather
crackles
and pops
as I do.
Because no one else does.
Someone loved
everyone
buried here—
they deserve to be
taken care of.
They shouldn't be forgotten.

Too many people who vanish
     (like the ones buried
     in the sugarcane fields
     of my mother's dark dreams)
disappear from our memories too.

I want to ask
if part of Benjamin
is sleeping somewhere
under my feet,
but I plaster my tongue
to the roof of my mouth.
Asking him
where his death is hidden
when we've only just met
would be cruel.

If I were a ghost,
I wouldn't like to be reminded of it,
especially
by someone whose heart
still flashes with life
under her shirt.

(I wouldn't like
          to be reminded
                              about my death
                                        at all.)

Benjamin
sits down next to me,
gripping his ankles tightly,
as if my breath
might send his soul
sailing far from Prague.
He's close enough now
that if he were ordinary,
I could trace
the sharp curve
of his jaw,
and smell the sweat
and earth
on his skin.

But Benjamin
is negative space

where a boy should be,
and he hunches his shoulders
up to his ears.
Why is he trying
to make himself smaller
when he's barely
a whisper
in this world as it is?

No one ever comes here, he says.
Not until you.
I thought they all wanted to forget.
I thought they'd succeeded.

They?
I edge
just a little closer.

The neighbors.
The people of Prague.
The living.
Why do you want
to remember the dead
when they aren't even yours?

Laughter grows inside me
the way the rose grows
from Benjamin.

I'm Jewish—
we're good at remembering.
We're asked to
in every prayer,
every candle we light,
every line of Torah.

The dead boy says:
Zochreinu l'chayim,
like we've both
been singing the lyrics
to the very same song.

I run my fingers
along the chipped base
of the matzevah closest to me.
Does anyone remember you, Benjamin?
Does your family still live near Rose Hill?
It's as close to his death
as I can make myself go.

Benjamin shakes his head.
I barely remember them,
but I know they're gone.
I'm the last one
left in Prague.
But it's for the best.
My family never had to see
the worst of what happened

to our cemetery,
to our city.

You could go too, I say.
You could follow them.
Maybe
I could help you
find them.
Maybe—

No!
Benjamin jumps up,
his rose turning black
with sudden rot.
You shouldn't even be here—
it was a mistake
for me to come back!

Why?
It's only a cemetery.
It's peaceful here.
Isn't it?

Benjamin's eyes
move like a rabbit's,
the pupils swollen
with fear.
I have to go.
I'm sorry.

Wait!
I reach for him,
even though I won't be able
to touch him.

But Benjamin is gone
and I am left
alone
      again,
heartstrings humming
with his absence.

I want to clean Benjamin's grave,
lay a stone there for him.

     (Flowers
     would wither
     and fade.
     A stone is eternal—
     like memory,
     like love.)

But how can I honor
a disappearing boy
when I don't even know
where he's buried?

Interlude I:
Wassermann

I was born a *vodník*,
the prince of rivers,
the keeper of drowned souls.

My first river
was the Danube.
She danced
through the Kingdom of Bavaria
and the nation of Hungary,
so beautiful
that men composed waltzes
inspired by
her jeweled waters.

Each day,
I fished the souls of the dead
from her current
and drank them with my tea.

Most humans
avoided me.
But there was one
who sought me out—
a rabbi, in the city of Ulm.
He begged me
to release the souls
I had captured.
And I
(so young, so foolish)
laughed at him!

The dead
I took from the water
tasted sweeter than pomegranates.
Why would I ever
part with them?

But I should have known
only a magician
would dare to approach me.

When I refused him,
the rabbi cast me
out of Ulm
and Bavaria.
He bound me
to a distant river—

the Vltava
in Prague.

The rabbi's magic
held me fast.
I could not leave
the city of a hundred spires.

After my exile,
I tried to craft myself
into something almost mortal.
I vowed
to be on my best behavior.
Only then,
I thought,
could I avoid
being sent into exile again.

I feigned humanity,
went to university,
attempted to turn
my appetites
to poetry,
polynomial equations,
and dentistry,
to fill the gaping hole
in my belly.

But I couldn't
deny myself forever.

It started
so small.
I stole pinches,
mouthfuls of people
who drowned in the river—
a memory here,
the name
of a once-beloved pet there,
just so there was
a little color
in my cheeks,
just enough
to drive away
the emptiness
inside me.

Yet my hunger
ate at me
until I could hold back
no longer.
I found the dead
(as I always do)
and coaxed them,
one by one,
into a house
of my own making.

Who were the dead?
Why,
the Jewish children
of Prague.
I couldn't very well
let the rabbi
go unpunished,
now could I?

This is the lesson
all monsters
must learn:
one's appetite
wins out
every time.
You can live
without love,
without a home,
without a river
if you are full
of something else.

Second Movement:
The Boy on the Hill

Chapter Ten

I dream about men
wandering the streets of Prague,
their lantern-eyes alight.
The wind doesn't stir
their coats;
their throats barely flash
as they breathe.

I can't see
the faces of these men.
I don't have to.
I can recognize
my family's monsters
      (of the past
            the present
                 the future)
even when I'm asleep.

Sarah and Martina
don't respond to my messages
for days.
Anxiety whittles me down
until I am small enough
to fit inside a teacup
and I've convinced myself
they've forgotten
I even exist.

Maybe
I don't.
Maybe Prague
is in another dimension
where the walls are made of ivy
and there's no difference
between the living
and the dead.

On Shabbat,
Sarah (finally)
sends me photos of her and Martina
posing on the beach,
their mouths puckered at the camera,
seeking a kiss.

Sarah tells me:
We wish you were here!

We're having so much fun!
Summer's not the same
without you!

I shove my phone
back into my pocket;
I wish I could throw it
into the river instead.
Jealousy
tastes bitter,
a mouthful of wormwood
or dead flowers.

There isn't anything
I can send Sarah
that wouldn't make me
look pathetic.
I have no pictures of myself
at a club, or with a beer,
standing beside
a group of friends
who will carry
the memory of me
and the scorching June
we spent together
for years to come.

I'm alone;
only secrets
keep me company.

Aunt Žofie's art
lives in a gallery
unlike any other
I've been to.

The building is narrow;
a spiral staircase
winds up the center,
like the spine of a giant.
Papier-mâché flowers
bloom from the walls
and there are paintings
tucked away
in every corner.
Some of the art
even spills out
onto the warped floorboards,
a wave
no one
            (not even my aunt)
can contain.

I walk through the gallery
while Aunt Žofie laughs

and bargains
with the khaki-clad tourists
the wind has blown
through her door.

They're always Americans
trying to own a bit of Prague.
They must believe
they can cram the city
into their suitcases
and bring it home with them.

But no one
can own magic.

In the worlds Žofie paints,
queens with black owl eyes
dance on bone-thin branches.
Satyrs with goat legs
steer leaf boats
across the many waters of Prague.
Witches float
in crystal spaceships
winking in
and out of the dark.

Longing swells in me
like a bubble.

I wish I could fill my days
    (and years)
with what I've created too.

The more paintings I see,
the more I start to realize
the same figure
appears in every one.

The man is barely there,
a nightmare left unfinished,
chased away by the dawn
and dreams of springtime.
But he stands out on each canvas,
a living scar.
He has no face,
only crooked teeth
and fox-bright eyes,
bottomless
with hunger.

Maybe he's a metaphor—
for poverty,
or all the monsters
    shaped like men
my aunt has seen.
But he feels too *real*.
There's a texture to this creature

that can't be found
in any dream.

Maybe Benjamin
isn't the only piece
of true magic
hovering on the edge
of Aunt Žofie's life.

What tears me away from the paintings
is the sound of a violin
playing high above me.
I creep
toward the stairs,
ears attuned
to the bombastic scales of Beethoven.

I'm not the only one listening.
From the corner of my eye,
I see a flash of a girl
in a dress
the color of strawberries—
the same girl from the café.

She gives me
a wild look
and runs up the stairs,
faster

than any child
has the right to be.

I follow the strawberry girl
and the trail of
          (dying)
flower petals
raining from her skin,
from her *soul*.
My braid slaps my neck,
urging me on.
I have to catch her;
I have to talk to her.

I reach the final step
on the second floor,
but I'm too late.
The music stops
and the strawberry girl
melts away,
a drop of water
pulled into
a much greater sea.

But someone else
is waiting for me.

          (Will I ever really be alone
          in my father's city?)

Chapter Eleven

Ilana!
We meet again!
Rudolf Wassermann
sets his black violin down
and claps his hands together
like he's just been given
a birthday present.

The paintings around him
look strangely dim,
their colors muted
by the glaring yellow of Wassermann's suit.
His shoes are wet;
they drip rudely onto the floor
where the man's shadow
should be,
turning the space tar black.

I know better than to ask
if he paid
to come inside the gallery.
I don't think he's paid
for anything
in years.

A creature can get away
with almost anything
if they only move
along the ragged edges of the world.

I ask Wassermann:
Where did the little girl go?

Wassermann's gaze
sweeps over me like a paintbrush.
Oh, you mean Pearl?
She's gone home.

Where's home?
It's a simple question,
but one most of my family
wouldn't be able to answer
honestly.
There are too *many* answers—
>Prague,
>Cuba,
>Miami,

nowhere
and everywhere.

Why, the house
where I met you!
It's one of Old Town's finest.

Wassermann whistles again
      (Waltz in A-Flat Major
      by Brahms)
as he walks his fingers
across the black violin's bridge.
The veins that show
through the skin of his wrists
are silver—
proof that Wassermann isn't like me
or anyone else.

I don't know why,
but I'm a little jealous of the man
with no shadow.
He always seems
stuffed
full
of beautiful things.

When did you start
playing the violin? I ask.
You're very good.

Oh,
when I was much,
much younger.
I'm older than I look, you see.
Though I hardly fit

into the world of grown-ups.
Wassermann grins,
showing off
his ridiculous teeth.

> (I like that they're flawed.
> Everyone should have
> at least one imperfection.)

What do you hope to be
when you grow up, Ilana?
An artist?
Or something else?

His question
feels loaded,
like a gun.
Whenever my parents
ask me
the same thing,
they're always disappointed
by my answer.

But Wassermann
has no interest
in degrees and salaries;
he doesn't fear
an empty bank account.

He'd have to be human
to care about those things
and he's anything *but.*

I want to be a violinist, **I say.**
I want to compose.
I want to be surrounded by music
every hour, every day.
But that's as impossible
as my old wish.
When I was little,
I wanted to be a mermaid.

Wassermann winks,
his smile
stretching even wider.
Perhaps
it's not as impossible
as you may believe.
There's already something
about the ocean in you,
and Prague has a river
that would love for you
to call it home.

I'd be a better mermaid
than I am a girl, I laugh.
But my parents

wouldn't allow that
any more than they'd let me
make music for a living.

Wassermann bows his head.
It's such a pity
some people don't appreciate
your love of music.
But there are those—
myself among them—
who understand
that music is life.
Without songs,
we'd surely choke
on the ugly, brittle pieces
of the world.
Don't you agree?

He didn't need to ask.
I'd already started nodding
when he'd barely begun.

Would you like to play?
Wassermann holds
the black violin out—
a gift,
a curse
I can't refuse,

even if I know
I should.

I take the instrument from him.
It fits perfectly
under my chin,
as if it were meant to be there—
meant to be *mine*.

The murmur of the bow
against the strings
reminds me:
I don't have to be a girl
uprooted from my country,
tied down by the knots
of other people's expectations.

I can be
so much bigger than that,
and I am
as I start to play.

I'm in the major key.
I'm E sharps, D minors.
I'm a crescendo
building toward something furious.
I picture my bones unraveling
like ribbons,

my hair
dissolving in the sunlight,
my soul
rising
up
out of my skin.

Reaching
the final note of my song
feels like falling
from the stars.
But I don't have time to mourn
my return to earth.

The man with no shadow
clutches one hand
over his heart.
The other
goes to his milky eye,
wiping away a tear.
If you're ever looking
for a teacher,
I'd be happy to be yours.
And you already play
so beautifully, Ilana.

I eat up Wassermann's praise
            (in spite of myself)

the way he devoured
my music.
Thank you.

The memory of the future
my parents decided for me
still hangs around my neck
like a stone.

But why shouldn't I accept
Wassermann's offer?
I have the whole summer.
I can study,
work in the cemetery,
and still
play music.

I recognize the tinny sound
made by Aunt Žofie's
pink high heels
clicking
on the iron staircase.
She calls out:
Ilana?
Are you up there?
I thought
I heard music.

But when she reaches the landing,
the wet impressions
of Wassermann's shoes
are all that's left of him.

Aunt Žofie looks at the little puddle
beneath her painting
of Libuše the prophetess.
Did you spill something?

I shake my head,
my truth
hidden under my tongue
like a candy.
No. I don't know
where the water came from.

Chapter Twelve

At first light,
I return to the cemetery,
shaking off new
        (and unsettling)
dreams of a man
stealing
strawberries from a garden
that won't ever be his.

My dreams
don't make sense
anymore.
But neither
does the waking world.

Benjamin isn't in the graveyard.
Disappointment
weighs me down
until I feel as heavy
as the gray waves of *matzevot*.

I want to run back to Rose Cottage.
My books are waiting for me;
I'll never earn
the test score I need
unless I start studying.
But the headstones
look so lonely;
I can't leave them like this.

My work goes slowly.
I can't tear the weeds free
without disturbing the
        (hallowed)
ground.
I trim the plants
as close to the earth as I can,

cursing
their prickled spines
and stubbornness.

But I don't stop.

We Jews call our cemeteries
beit chayyim—
        the house of the living,
beit shalom—
        the house of peace.

This place
was,
is,
always will be
        sacred,
even if
the only visitors
are the bluebird choirs
in the birch trees
and one living girl.

Benjamin's arrival
is fox-quiet.
He sits down beside me,
crossing one leg
over the other.

The light pours through him,
as if he's made of lace.

I'm sorry
about the other day, Benjamin says.
Running away was childish.
I wasn't sure
if I could trust you.
But you're taking care
of the cemetery.
That says so much
about your heart—
and your intentions.

I would never do anything
to hurt this place
or the memory
of the people here, I reply.
I just want to help.

But I think
Benjamin feared more
than what my intentions might be.

There's a secret
hanging around him
like a cloud of smoke.
It clings to

every strand of Benjamin's hair
and the folds of his clothes.

What reason could a dead boy have
to be so scared?
Does he think
he'll be forced to move on
if I tend to the cemetery
like a garden?

Or is something else
troubling him,
        some greater shadow
I haven't learned
how to see?

Benjamin unfolds
a loose collection of pages
from his pockets
and spreads them across his lap.
Each calls to me
as songs have in the past.
I'm
        (only half)
surprised to see
he's an artist.

His paintings are made of unearthly colors.
I want to press each
into my heart.

I ask Benjamin:
How can you paint like this?
Can you imagine
things into existence?

Benjamin guides his hand
down one of the pages.
There's a place I go
where I can eat and drink
and hold a paintbrush
in my hands.
There's a place I go
where I can almost
be alive.

Olam Ha-Ba? I ask.
The World to Come?

The blue-eyed boy goes still.
I've never been there.
It's still to come
for me.

Then Benjamin
purses his lips and silence
submerges us
once again.

The ghost
riffles through his art,
skipping past certain pages.
But I blush
when I catch a glimpse of a drawing
he tries to hide.
      Because
          it's
               of *me*.

I'm not beautiful enough
to be anyone's inspiration,
but when formed
by Benjamin's hand,
I look mythical.

No one has ever seen me
like *that*—
let alone a boy.
I'm no afterthought with him;
I'm fully present in his (after) life
and he is present
in mine.

He has a favorite subject,
this lost boy of wonders:
Prague.

Angels fill
the sharp blue skies of Benjamin's city.
Rabbi Loew's golem
stalks the streets,
his eyes burning with furious
            and just
intentions.

An author sits
hunched over a typewriter
with Hebrew letters
printed on its keys.
Cockroaches scuttle
across his feet.
The insects
have the same sad look
as the writer himself.

The Vltava isn't friendly
in Benjamin's Prague.
The river
cleaves his city
in two,
a black knife.

Wicked mermaids,
rusalki from Aunt Žofie's gruesome,
ancient tales
gather on the shorelines,
murderous as crows.
They smile, exposing
double rows of white shark teeth.

They don't hide anything from me.
We're all girls;
we know our softness conceals
what's most merciless about us.

Benjamin's art
reminds me of the pale figure
haunting
Aunt Žofie's paintings.
His brushstroke beasts are lively
        (like hers)
and every street
hides
a nest of monsters.

I don't know if I want to live
in Benjamin's Prague.
But I don't think
I have much of a choice.

Is all of this real? I ask.

I wish the angels were
and the rusalki weren't, Benjamin says.
And my zayde
swore up and down
he'd seen the remains of the golem
in Staronová synagoga's attic.
He said
we should have buried it
in the cemetery,
along with old Torah scrolls,
because Rabbi Loew
wrote the name of God
on its forehead.

Benjamin pauses,
a small smile
          (lost somewhere
                    between my life
                              and his death)
taking shape
on his lips.
I'd forgotten
about all the strange things
Zayde used to tell me.
Like how birds
sang about the future,

if you just listened hard enough.
I don't know if he was right.
But I used to feed them anyway.

I say:
I feed stray cats
by the shoreline where I live.
Maybe they're like your grandfather's birds
and can read the future
in the cowrie shells
that wash up on the beach.
But even if they can,
they'll never reveal
what they see.
Cats enjoy mysteries
a little too much
to give away anybody's ending.

What else do you do at home?
Benjamin asks.
He speaks more freely now,
his fear
        (of what—
        or of who?)
melting away
in the sun.

I shrug.

I play music.
I swim in the sea.
I spend time
with my friends.
I fight
with my parents.
I dream
about monsters.
What else do you do
when you're sixteen?

I did the same things
when I was alive, says Benjamin.
I do almost the same things
now that I'm sixteen forever.
It's good to know
not everything in the world
has changed.

Chapter Thirteen

It's the strangeness of Benjamin and me
that makes me speak my truth.
If we can talk about magic,
we should be able
to talk about *anything*.

My parents
don't want me to become a violinist.
That's what we fight about—
what we always fight about.

They want me to grow up
to be practical,
and musicians
are anything but.
We do everything
with our hearts
and nothing
with our heads.

They want me
to make money
the way only
engineers,
doctors,
and lawyers
can.
They're afraid
I'll wind up
where they started
when they first arrived
in America—
with nothing.

And now they've made me afraid
of the future too.

A new rosebud
breaks open
on the back of Benjamin's hand,
a thoughtful
frosty white.
He's made of too much earth,
not enough boy.

I know how that feels, he whispers.
I wanted to sketch, paint, sculpt.
I wanted to be like Alphonse Mucha
and make the world brighter,
more extraordinary.
I wanted to bring gardens
to those
who couldn't grow flowers themselves.

But my father
wanted me to become a doctor,
to heal the world
with skills that meant
I'd never go hungry.

So I studied from dawn
until the last star

left the sky,
trying not to think
about going to medical school
in Vienna
as I sketched my dreams
in the margins of my textbooks.

I dare
to lean closer to him.
Then what happened?

Benjamin's rose
darkens.
I died
before my father and I
could settle the argument.

Everyone's story is supposed to end
with a death.
There's something so sad
about how Benjamin's *didn't.*
He exists at the second to last page,
the eleventh hour,
the twilight
of his self.

He never gets to close the book,
he just *is—*

stranded,
    timeless,
unable to be
one thing
or the other.

It's this thought
that seizes me in its jaws
when Benjamin passes his hand
over mine.
The feel of him is so cold
it burns.

I let it.

I spend the rest of the morning
talking with Benjamin
as I untangle the ivy
from a group of *matzevot*,
    (the names
    on the stones
    faded
    beneath wind, rain, time)
until the heat of the noon sun
urges me
inside Rose Cottage.

I invite Benjamin along.
He declines,
but I know
he'll be back.

What kind of song
would I use
to capture Benjamin's likeness?
Would he be a waltz,
moving slowly
over the face of the world?
Or a sonata,
lonely and caught
in a spell
of his own making?

I can't decide.
But magic
isn't meant to be captured
by anyone.
It would be like locking a sunbeam
inside a glass jar.

Maybe magic
is just meant to *be*.

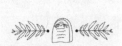

Chapter Fourteen

As I scrub the cemetery dirt
off my hands,
I hear a knock at the door.
It carries through the house
like a shout.

I don't have time
to take off my red sneakers;
they leave dusty prints
on the old wood floorboards
as I run to the front of the cottage.

By the time I open the door,
whoever was there
is gone.
But they left something behind:
a box
wrapped in plain brown paper
tied with a cord.

I carry it inside, searching
for a note or card
tucked
under the string.

It could have come
from anyone;
it could be
for anyone.

    (But deep
    down
    I know
    it's for *me*.)

I tear the paper off the box,
    hands
           shaking,
and lift the lid.

Inside, Wassermann's black violin rests
like a sleeping cat,
begging to be touched.

I see my reflection
in the instrument's resinous wood,
the skin of a black pine
felled decades ago.
In its darkness,
I could almost be pretty,
the girl Benjamin drew
with such care.

Gently,
I raise the violin
up to the light.
I shouldn't play it;
it doesn't belong to me.
But I haven't
had an instrument of my own
since I came to Prague.

Someone
who loves songs
made this.
      Someone
            like
                  me.

My fingers find
all the right strings
and I pick up my feet
to dance.

My parents
didn't steal my music.
It was hidden away,
waiting
in the bridge of the black violin
for me
to call it home.

This is how Aunt Žofie finds me,
twirling around the kitchen,
my red shoes blurring beneath me.
I move so fast
I don't think I can stop
until she grabs my arm.

The bow
slips
off the strings,
leaving us in silence so ugly
I want to scream.

Aunt Žofie plucks the violin
out of my hands.
What are you doing?
Where did you get this?
She sounds as frantic
as my dancing.

Someone
left it at the door.
There's a sharp edge to every syllable;
I'm more wolf
than girl.

Aunt Žofie's frown
is grave deep.

It must have been delivered
to the wrong address.
I hope the real owner
finds out that we have it soon.
I'll put it in my studio
until they come for it.

She's wrong—
this isn't a mistake.
Wassermann said
he wanted to hear my music
and be my teacher.
Now he can do both.

Chapter Fifteen

Everyone else my age
sneaks cigarettes,
gulps of wine,
kisses with the wrong person.
My rebellion is different:
I've started sneaking songs.

Whenever Aunt Žofie
goes to the shop,
the gallery,

the bank,
I pull the black violin
out from under her easel,
and lose myself
in music.

I play Beethoven,
Schubert,
Mozart,
Philip Glass,
Jorge Grundman.

I play until my hands throb
more than they do
when I've done battle
with the cemetery's forest.

I'm getting away with something—
giving in
to an addiction.

And I don't ever want to stop.

I'm becoming a more skilled violinist
by the hour.
My notes are cleaner, sharper;
they move faster
than light.

But better than the music I play
is the music I *compose*.

Berceuses, nocturnes,
sonatas blossom
from my fingers,
the way roses do
from Benjamin's veins.

I record
one of my new compositions
for Sarah and Martina.
The quality of the audio is poor;
but I can still read the envy
between each word of Martina's response:

> *You've gotten even better—*
> *what happened?*

I tell her:

> *It's quiet here;*
> *I can hear the music*
> *even when I'm not playing.*

My friends
don't know what to make of that.
They fall silent,
somewhere in Miami.

> (Again.)

Joy is honey-sweet in my mouth
when I tell Benjamin
about the music.
I haven't wanted to compose
in months!
All I could ever think about
was how my parents wouldn't approve.
But now
everything's different.
I'm so happy
the man with no shadow
gave me his violin.

Benjamin tries to smile,
but his grin
shimmers
at the corners.

Why isn't he happier for me?
I put my hand over his
and don't shiver when his fingers
     cold
     as November rain
pass through mine.
     (I wish
     they wouldn't.
     I wish
     I could hold his hand
     and feel it properly.)

Don't worry.
As long as I'm in Prague,
I'll always come here
to take care of the cemetery
and be with you, I say.

I know.
But Benjamin's words
sound like a nocturne,
tinged
with too many shades of regret.

Chapter Sixteen

The ivy
I've freed the *matzevot* from
lies in a heap.
It looks like the sort of thread
Aunt Žofie's fairies
use to make their dresses.

But I have no need
for magical fabric today.
I've taken my exam books
up to Rose Hill;
I can think more clearly here

than anywhere else in the world.
Maybe some of that magic
will extend to my studies.

I wipe my grimy hand
on a page instructing me
how to decode
SAT word problems.
I read aloud:
According to this chart,
if 500 people,
        18 or older,
visited a museum in 2017,
approximately how many people
        in total
visited the museum in 2017?

Benjamin doesn't announce himself.
But when does he ever?
He greets me instead
with a question.
Which museum is it?

I glance up,
unsurprised that he's come.
Does that matter?

It does.
Benjamin steps
around the ivy.
> (Does it move a little
> when his ankle brushes against it?
> Or am I only dreaming?)

Everyone visits
the Mucha Museum
and the Kafka Museum.
But not many people
know about
the Museum of Alchemists.

When I ask him
what an alchemist is,
Benjamin beams.
A magician
who turns lead
into gold,
who finds potions to make kings
immortal.
Didn't you ever have alchemists
in America?

I learn more
from Benjamin's stories
than I ever have studying.

And they're so much more interesting
than the book I close
and put aside.

I spill my secrets like water
when I'm with my ghost.
Benjamin has made me bold,
along with the cemetery
　　　(less green,
　　　more itself
　　　with every passing day
　　　and every weed
　　　I trim)
and the return of my music.

But I still have to gather
all my courage
to ask him:
Which headstone is yours?

The boy dusts off his trousers.
Today I can see
a little less of the sky
through him.
He doesn't feel
like an echo
of what was
and never can be again.

I follow Benjamin to a *matzevah*
sheltered by an old elm.
A crack
races
across the willow tree
carved on it.
One of its branches is broken in half,
the sign of a life
cut short.

This one, says Benjamin.
He runs his fingers
across the *matzevah*.
They part the curtain of ivy
and he pulls back abruptly,
shock
stealing the color
from his already pale face.

We look at each other,
but can't find the words
to describe what we have just seen:
a dead boy
reaching
into the land of the living.

Instead, I read the inscription
    (*Benjamin ben Aaron,*
    may his soul
    be bound up
    in the bond of eternal life)
on the headstone and wish
I could whisper
Benjamin back into this world
for more than just a moment.
I'll take care of your grave.
I promise.

I snap photos of the cemetery.
I even attempt to capture Benjamin
in one of the pictures.
But he appears
as nothing more
than a glimmer
at the edge of the frame.

I try to explain to Sarah and Martina
what the cemetery
means to me
    (what *Benjamin* means to me)
but the words
stick to the back of my throat
and the ends of my fingertips.

I can hear Sarah's gasp
when she types:

> *These pictures are so creepy!*
> *Where are you?*

I can hear Martina's disbelieving laugh
when she asks me:

> *Seen any ghosts?*

I know my friends—
they don't think about the shapes souls take
or what happens to them
after.
They live in a world
where flowers can't blossom
from a lost boy
and love is concrete,
proven
with a touch
or a kiss.

I settle for white lies.
It's just me here—
but history is all around me.

By the beginning of July,
there's a space between me
and my clothes
that wasn't there before.

Aunt Žofie slips her finger
into this new void
where my skin
used to ride up against my jeans.
I know girls are obsessed
with thinness.
But—

I don't let her finish.
She needs to know
I'm not trying
to wear myself down.

It's not like that. It must be the work
I'm doing in the cemetery.
I'm eating more than ever.

And I am.
I'm hungry
all
the
time.
My belly is hollow,
the way I felt all over
before I took my music back.

I'll eat anything—
pinches of day-old bread,

bags of potato chips
dusted with paprika.
I suck down strawberries
until my fingers and jaw
are a murderous red.

But instead of swelling outward,
I'm collapsing inward,
a black hole
of a girl.

It's almost enough
to frighten me.

But music never stole from me before.
I have to trust it
and the gift
Rudolf Wassermann put back
in my hands.

Chapter Seventeen

Unlike my parents,
Benjamin only stops me from playing music
when I bring the black violin
to the cemetery's borders.

He tries to take the instrument
out of my hands
before I can even raise
the bow to the strings.

Dance with me! Benjamin pleads.
Play an American song—
something cheerful,
something that makes me want to soar
instead of cry.
I haven't danced
with anyone in years;
I can't forget how to—
and I almost have.
Dancing
was one of the best parts
of living.

How can I say no to that?
It would be the greatest tragedy of all
if a boy like Benjamin
forgot how to dance.

I set aside the black violin
and pick up my phone instead,
scrolling through track after track
until I find a song bubbly enough
to satisfy Benjamin.

We spin
around and around on Rose Hill,
carried aloof
by the gentle waves of music
as I usually am
by the sea.
Our grins flash like stars
crossing
an ink-toned sky.
Our laughter is unafraid;
it moves between worlds,
places our hands can't go.
We don't care who sees us.

     (If anyone even can.)

I'm terrible!
Benjamin says—and he is.
I can tell he never grew into his feet.
He trips over them,
the way I trip
over loose stones.

I'm worse! I call back.
     (This is how you know
     you're close to someone.
     When you can
     insult yourself

and they'll do the same,
just to soften the blow
of your truth.)

The two of us dance
until I'm breathless
and he pretends to be.
We collapse
on the velvet-soft grass,
our laughter drifting in wisps
up to the clouds.

We escape afterward,
into the city
that's both an adventure
and a cage,
depending on the day,
the decade,
the century.

I swing my arms at my sides
as we walk toward the river,
hoping my fingers
will graze Benjamin's
accidentally,
on purpose.

I don't know why
I want to touch him all the time.
It's like I need to confirm
Benjamin is real
because I haven't been
this close to anyone
ever.

      (Let alone a boy.)

I haven't acted like a tourist
since I arrived.
Gawking at this city
feels strange
when it's only by chance
I didn't grow up here myself.
It must be stranger still for Benjamin,
who has seen Prague
change her clothes, her hair,
her outlines and curves
so many times
she might as well be
someone new.

We step into a puppeteer's shop
along with people
chattering like sparrows
in English, German, French.

Marionettes dangle from the ceiling:
goblins and aristocrats made of elm,
Charlie Chaplins and witches,
princesses with faded-sky wings.
They're all equal here
in this magical kingdom.

Puppets, like the rest of Prague,
have decided on democracy.

Benjamin bumps against a princess
in summer blue.
She shakes wildly on her strings,
as if she couldn't resist dancing
for such a beautiful boy.
He gasps,
surprised
by his own ability to change
the world.

(I'm a little surprised myself.)

The shopkeeper looks over,
his face already crinkled
in displeasure,
ready to banish me
with a flick of his hand
for mishandling his creations.

But I'm too far away
to have moved the marionette,
and he returns to work
with a shrug, grumbling:
It was only the wind.

(How many times
has he repeated that lie?
How many ghosts
have passed through this shop?)

I bite my lip,
holding back a laugh.
And beside me, Benjamin
clamps a hand
over his own mouth.

I whisper:
Let's go
before our shared giggles
have the chance to bubble up.

Chapter Eighteen

How many other ghosts
like you are there? I ask Benjamin.
It's an idea that can only

be raised in sunlight.
Dead children
don't make for polite conversation.
Like the strawberry girl—
Pearl.

Benjamin looks away from me.
There aren't as many hauntings
as you might think.
It's just Pearl, myself,
and two other boys—
both younger
than I am.

When did they ...?
I can't bring myself to finish
the question.

The twins died
a few months after I did, taken
by the flu in 1918.
Pearl was lost
during the war.
Prague doesn't try to cling
to its dead.
We're only still here because ...
Benjamin's mouth
snaps
shut,

a door being slammed
by an angry hand.

Because? I prompt.

But Benjamin
shakes his head
and walks ahead of me,
his expression
masked
by the glare of the sunlight.

Whatever unfinished business
that binds Benjamin
to this city
belongs to him—
and him alone.
He doesn't need to share it
with me.

But how much he conceals
still worries me.
I tell him *everything*.
What isn't
he telling *me*?

I buy a *trdelník*
from a street vendor,
fighting against my growling belly.

Instead of a papery cone,
my ice cream is wrapped in cinnamon dough.
It coats my fingers with brown sugar,
like pixie dust.

I offer it to Benjamin
before I remember
he can't share it with me.
He smiles nonetheless,
his eyes lost
in the waves of his dimples.
I'm relieved
Benjamin looks like a boy again,
and not
a collection of secrets.

    (Maybe he just likes his privacy.
    Maybe I am looking for darkness
    where there is none.)

Benjamin says:
How long will you stay with your aunt?
Or will you live here from now on?

Does he sound hopeful?
I'd like to think
he wants me by his side
as much as I want him

by mine.
But I have to tell him
the truth.
I'll be gone by September.
I have to go back to school
in Miami.
And my father hates Prague—
he'd never let me stay.

But August
seems like a lifetime away
and I don't want to go back
to a home
that fits me poorly,
a pair of sandals
I've long outgrown.
Not when I've only just reclaimed
my music
and made a friend
like Benjamin.

My simplest daydreams
become the biggest lies of all.

I dream
I can bring Benjamin
back to Miami with me,
as if he's a postcard.

I dream
he can walk the halls
of my high school,
study art in New York,
open a gallery someday
like my aunt.

I dream
we can grow up
and grow old
together,
sharing our hearts,
inside jokes,
decades.

Is that what he would want,
if it were possible?

The cold ice cream
sets my mouth aflame
when I sink my teeth into it.
You were scared to talk to me
at first.
Why?
> (I need to ask:
> I need to know.)

Benjamin worries his lip
between his teeth.
When he speaks again,
his voice is hoarse,
as if it's coming
from a great distance.
Herr Wassermann
prefers the other children and me
not to talk to strangers
or go too far from his house.
I stay with him,
so I must respect
his rules.

I suck the last of the strawberry ice cream
off my fingers,
trying to draw out the sweetness.
                    (I already want more.)
You live with Rudolf Wassermann?
The same Wassermann
who gave me the violin?

I do.
Me …
and the other three children.
But Wassermann
isn't dead like us.
I don't think

he's ever died.
I don't think
he ever will.

Is that a comfort
or a curse?
It's hard to say.
Why didn't you tell me
you knew Wassermann?

Benjamin shrugs,
stuffing his hands
into the pockets of his trousers.
I'm so used to keeping secrets.
It's a habit
I'm finding
hard to break.

Chapter Nineteen

Benjamin and I don't cross Charles Bridge
to reach Staroměstské náměstí:
the Old Town Square.
It's too crowded
with tourists,
their elbows sharp,
and their English sharper.

Benjamin takes me over the other bridge—
the one that's too plain
for anyone to care about.
No statues guard it
and cars speed past,
reminding us
what year it is.

I call this one
the Quiet Bridge, I say.
I don't know the real name.

The smile Benjamin gifts me with
is golden.
I like "Quiet Bridge"
better than its real name.
It sounds much more magical.
Like a place a good queen
might make her home.

You talk about magic all the time.
Is it easier to believe in it
when you're magic yourself? I ask.

Benjamin
closes his eyes,
searching the world inside of him.
I think it's harder.

Because magic feels ordinary
and miracles
seem so far away.
You're more of a miracle
than I am.

I laugh—
I'm not that kind of girl.
How can you say
I'm a miracle?

You're a Jew.
You're alive in Prague
and you see me.
You see everything.
Why isn't that a miracle?

The buildings on the other side of Quiet Bridge
lean into each other,
gossips interested
in the sight of Benjamin and me,
the living and the dead
gathered so close together.

But the tourists and shopkeepers
don't question
the presence of a teenage girl,
her hand

wrapped around nothing
but the warm summer air.

Every wall,
brick,
stone
tells a story,
and Benjamin
can read them all.

He places
his hands
over the bullet holes
scarring
the nearest building's façade.
There was a fight here,
at the end of the war.
The people of Prague
finally pushed back
against the Nazis.
They even
managed to win.

Of course Benjamin was here,
watching that last struggle.
He must have been here
for almost everything.
Did you cheer for them?

Benjamin nods.
The rose
sprouting from his cheek
is a blue
far deeper
than the waters of the Vltava.
I did.
But I wish
they had fought back sooner.
I wish
they could have risen up
the day the Germans
first marched into the city.
And I wish
I could have risen up
beside them.

My whole face turns
the color of
strawberry ice cream
the longer I watch Benjamin.

I want to stroke his hair,
the way I caress
the black violin's
slender neck.

He's talking
about war;
I'm thinking
about nonsense.
      What's wrong
               with me?

We haven't gone far
when Benjamin grabs at my arm,
trying to wrench me back
from whatever mistake
I'm about to make.
Ilana, please!
Please don't walk on them.

His eyes look like clouds
about to break open
with rain
as he points to the sidewalk.
Below you.
It's …

I reach down;
the marble stones
warm the starfish of my fingers.
I'm about to ask Benjamin
why he's so upset
when I see it for myself.

There are Hebrew letters
etched on the pathway.
They are even more faded
than the writing
in Rose Hill's cemetery.
These are *matzevot*
and people walk over them daily,
oblivious
to their meaning.

Who did this? I whisper.
Was it the Nazis?

No, says Benjamin.
It was the communists.
They needed building material
and there were no other stones
to be found.
So they took the matzevot *from a village*
and laid them here.
They said
it didn't matter,
because there was no one left
to care for that cemetery
or the people in it.

I never expected
Benjamin and me

to have monsters in common.
Years and oceans separate us,
and only half my family
claims this city as their own.
But the communists
stole from him too.

I'm sorry, I tell Benjamin,
as if I'm the one
who ripped up the headstones
and planted them here
like a briar patch.
This isn't right.
Someone
should bring the headstones
back to their village.

It isn't right, says Benjamin.
But so many things here aren't.

Chapter Twenty

I wake to the sound of rain
pounding against the roof,
relentless and gray.
I won't be able to get anything done

in the cemetery,
but I still run up Rose Hill
in search of Benjamin.

Only the trees greet me;
ghosts must be mindful of the weather too.
A thorny vine of disappointment
snakes
through
the pit of my stomach.

I shouldn't rely on a boy
to fill the space inside me.
But Benjamin isn't just a boy—
he's my friend.
And slowly,
I feel him becoming
something more.

I follow Aunt Žofie to her gallery,
       (exam books in hand)
hoping
she believes it's the weather
making me quiet, sullen,
lost
in my own head.

I'm caged-tiger restless.
I flip through my study guides
for the first time in weeks,
but I can't concentrate.
The more I pace,
the more irritated I become
with my aunt's pretend worlds.

I'm tired of dreams;
I want something real
the way most people
crave sugar, coffee,
and other vices.

I tell Aunt Žofie
I need to stretch my legs
and am out the door
before she can give me
a reason to stay.

I need to know more
about Benjamin and Pearl,
about the forgotten world
they lived in.

I can think
of only one place
to start.

Inside the Pinkas Synagogue
    (built in 1535)
there are names
painted on the walls
in red and black ink.

They're a chapter
in the history of my People,
but I can't read them all.
There are too many—
    78,000
victims of the Nazis,
    Czechs and Slovaks
murdered, all because
    they were Jews.

This is what it's like to be Jewish
in Europe.
Every beautiful thing
has horror buried under it.

               I'm always walking on bones.

The rooms upstairs
are much worse.

Inside rows of glass cases
    (like coffins)

are drawings from the war.
Most of the children
who made them
didn't survive the Shoah;
only their watercolor fairy tales did.

The pictures
tell stories of lives
unfinished.
But one catches my eye
  (and my heart)
more than the others:
a drawing of a princess
in a tower, roses winding
through her long dark hair.
And the name of the child
who made it?
Pearl.

Did the little ghost draw this?
I don't know,
but now I wish
I'd never come here at all.

Dad and Aunt Žofie didn't warn me
about any of this.
I don't think they understood
they *needed* to.

The specter of a different darkness
hangs over
my father and aunt.

The tanks that rolled through this city
when *they* were children
arrived from
　　　Russia,
　　　Poland,
　　　Hungary,
not Germany.
Their enemies marched
under the banner of the hammer and sickle,
not the spider-shaped mark of the swastika.

What I inherited
from *both* of my parents:
a healthy fear
of men in uniform.

Chapter Twenty-One

I slip outside into the rain again,
feeling like half a ghost myself.
Because that's the other part
of being a Jew in Europe—

each step I take
is in defiance of everyone
who didn't want me here.

I should be angry,
but all I can feel is sadness
burrowing into my bones.

I think maybe
the anger
will roar to life
when I'm least expecting it to.

I walk to the Staronová synagoga,
the Old-New Synagogue,
hoping to find
evidence of Benjamin and Pearl
that isn't a funeral dirge.

Myths are locked
behind the walls of this place.
Twelve stone vines
for the twelve tribes of Israel
      (ten lost, with no bread crumbs
      to follow home)
scale the entryway.
Rabbi Loew's clay beast
may still be sleeping
in the attic.

The synagogue's so old
I can almost feel it breathe.
It's like a golem itself,
crowded with history
and holy things.

Inside, the glittering chandeliers
mimic the stars,
and the arch of the ceiling
is ancient and strong.

Did Benjamin pray here?
Did he welcome the Shabbat bride
through its doors?
Did he recite Kaddish
for the lost,
Mi Shebeirach
for the sick?

I try to picture him
standing in front of the ark,
his cheeks pink,
his chest rising up
and down
as he swayed in time
with his prayers.

Thinking about what he was like
when he was alive
is so much better
than thinking about his end—
however it came,
whatever form it took.

There is a cemetery
behind the synagogue,
where the *matzevot* huddle together,
bracing for a storm.

I circle the graves.
I recognize all the carvings now:
lions and candelabras,
hands and crowns
and six-sided stars.

No one hacked down
the *matzevot* here
like they were trees
that needed to be felled.
This cemetery is intact, whole,
in a way that Benjamin's isn't.

Standing beneath a skeletal tree
at the rear of the cemetery
is none other

than Rudolf Wassermann,
umbrella in hand.
A cigarette
dangles from his mouth,
weeping ash
onto the broken pavement.

We stare at each other
above the forest of headstones.

You can't smoke in here, I say.
It's against the law.

Wassermann blinks.
The gesture looks forced,
like he's only now realizing
that he should.
Oh my! I'm so sorry.
He pinches the top of his cigarette
between two fingers
to extinguish it.

I gasp.
Wait—

But when the dead cigarette
falls from his hand,
there's no blister

or burn
left behind.
The fire doesn't mark
Rudolf Wassermann.

He asks:
*Would you like
to get out of the rain,
have a cup of tea with me?
This really isn't the weather
for sightseeing.*

    (I can't argue
    with that.)

Chapter Twenty-Two

The café Wassermann chooses is elegant.
The blue and gold spirals
painted on the walls
remind me of the synagogue
I just left.

Wassermann and I aren't followed
by the whisper of pens
and the flutter of paper

as he leads me
to the back of the café.
The room around us
is empty,
in spite of the *Reserved* signs
on almost every table.

Wassermann draws a chair back for me
and I sit,
letting the edges of the tablecloth
drape over my legs.
Even a hint of winter
is enough to make me shiver.

Benjamin lives with you.
It's a statement I open with,
not a question.
Pearl too.

Wassermann folds his hands,
forming one of the city's many spires.
Yes. They stay with me
when the sun goes down
and it's no longer safe
for children to walk the streets.
Starlight is cold
and one can't dine
on night air alone.

Ilana, you must understand—
the world has tried
to brush those children
off its coattails
and leave them
in the shadows.
I do what I can
for the souls
everyone else has forgotten.
Everyone …
except for you.
You like Benjamin,
don't you?

He's a good friend.
My voice is smooth
as buttercream,
betraying nothing.

A waiter
brings us *lipový čaj*,
linden tea,
in porcelain cups that were new
when Benjamin was still alive.

Wassermann
sips at his thoughtfully;
it brings a flush to his pale cheeks.

He has the look of a man
who's been on the brink
of illness
for a long time.

I think it's wonderful
you and Benjamin
have found each other, he says.
The other children
are so much younger than him!
He needed a friend
his own age.

The man with no shadow
leans forward suddenly,
a spy
about to impart a secret.
You must have received my violin.

It's beautiful, I say.
But I don't understand
why you've given it
to me.

Wassermann throws back his head,
laughing.
The entire world
must be a joke to someone

who just might live forever.
You can make music
whenever you like now.
Isn't that
what you wished for?

I want to believe
someone understands me effortlessly
           (the way Benjamin does)
and that Wassermann knows
I'm not a piece of music
too complicated
to be read,
the way my parents
believe I am.

Does it matter
if the creatures
who see the whole of me
aren't human
(anymore)?

The rain drums her fingers
on the café's gilded windows,
impatient
for me to return to Aunt Žofie.
She'll be wondering
where I am.

I've been gone
too long
already.

Thank you for the tea, I say.
And the conversation.

Before you go,
I have something else for you.
Wassermann takes several wrinkled pages
out of his coat pocket,
another gift
I can't repay him for.
"The Last Rose of Summer"
is one of the most difficult pieces
for violin.
But I know
you're capable of mastering it.

I gather the sheet music,
crushing it
against my chest.
I already want
to bring the song to life.
I'll do my best.

And you'll succeed.
Wassermann raises his cup,

a farewell toast.
You know where to find me—
and Benjamin.
Come see us anytime.
We both enjoy your company
so very much.

The battery on my phone
dips down
into warning yellow,
then desperate red.
It begs me to answer
the messages piling up,
letters from a past
I'm struggling
to connect with.

I spin lies
for my parents' benefit.
I tell them how much
I'm (not) studying,
how much thinking
I have (not) done
about my future.

I've stopped
sending photos to Sarah and Martina.
I don't care
      (anymore)

about whether or not
I see theirs.

No picture can explain
my descent into places
so dark they shimmer.

I leave my phone behind,
along with my exam books,
their pages dusty
thanks to my lack of attention.

I don't care.
I have better things to do.

Interlude II:
Wassermann

You can divide
the whole of the world
into two types of girls:
girls who say yes
and girls who say no.

I am only interested
in girls
who say yes.

Girls who say yes
become queens
ruling distant lands.
Songs
about their bravery
and beauty
will fall from the lips
of troubadours
for centuries.

Girls who say no
remain where they are,
stranded in the mud
and in the smallness of their villages.
They marry the baker's boy,
grow old and coarse.
And when
they finally crumble
beneath the weight of decades,
no one remembers them
for very long.

I have been
at the center
of so many tales
about girls who say yes.

I am
the wizard,
the fairy godfather,
the call to adventure
begging children
to leave home behind.
I am
the keeper of enchantment;
I snap my fingers
(fiat lux!)
and the light gathers around me
like so many fireflies.

Or so it used to.

My magic has faded,
my eyes have dimmed,
my stomach growls,
my bones *ache*.

The unfulfilled potential
bottled
in the souls of the four
dead children
who reside in my house
doesn't sate my hunger now.
I haven't had a decent supper
in *years*.

The children fade
a little more each day.
Soon,
they will disappear,
the last of them swallowed
not by me,
but by oblivion.

I've tried to find
more dead children,
their souls stuffed full
of bright wonders

and dreams of tomorrows
they'll never see.
They fill the hole in me,
as the souls of adults
(their hopes gone stale
with age)
never quite do.

But in the twenty-first century,
children are more likely
to grow up.
Vaccines,
peace,
simple human kindness
steal
countless
meals from me.

And boys and girls
with breath still in their lungs
refuse to follow me home.
They distrust
the crepuscular glow of my eyes,
my missing shadow,
the simple fact
that I am a stranger.

(I can hardly blame them.)

I need more, more, *more*.
But first,
I need company
with a heartbeat—
Ilana, the pretty girl
whose hunger
and love of music
matches my own.

If I can have her at my side,
I know I will not starve.
She can help me
fetch living children,
as her ancestors
fetched water from the Vltava.
They'll trust Ilana—
her longing,
her songs,
all the ways she's similar
to *them*.

Their memories,
their possibilities
will be enough
to sustain us both.
Even a girl
like Ilana
can become immortal

if she eats enough souls.
And who would turn down
eternity?

Together,
Ilana and I
are going to live
forever.

Chapter Twenty-Three

It's done.
There are no more branches to cut,
no more rotting leaves,
no more stinging nettles
masking their bite
with gentle purple flowers.
The cemetery is finally open
to the sky.

I tap
my hedge trimmers
against one ankle,
my skin dawn pink
and blistered from the nettles.

Benjamin traces
the mossy outline of a name
on one of the *matzevot*
before his hand
travels to the Torah crown
above it.
His name was Jan Lederer—
my teacher.

He was so old that he bent
like a willow in the wind.
We used to say
he helped Rabbi Loew
build the golem.

Who else is here
that you knew? I ask.

Benjamin's voice
becomes a grand map.
He lays out not streets
but lives,
dozens of red strings
that wrapped themselves
around his
(still)
beating heart.

We've walked halfway
across the cemetery
when the roses
on the backs of Benjamin's hands
wilt, as if the sun
has stolen
the last of their color.
It hurts to see;
they were so vivid

just a moment ago.
This must be boring,
hearing about
all these people
you'll never meet.

I tell him:
No.

I tell him:
Never.

I tell him:
I want to know everything.

A piece of Prague's magic

must come from its art museums,

and Benjamin

wants me to visit them all.

He whispers instructions

on how to punch my tram ticket

and which routes to take.

He shows me

the masters of his craft,

our feet making music

      (as his never did before)

on the marble floors of grand galleries.
We have a new mission now:
to see everything marvelous
in the city that Benjamin's bones
still call home.

Our minds
are alight
with beauty—
the blue diamond skyline,
the stained glass windows
with fairy tales
fitted into the panels.

I pose
beside a painted woman
      (*Princess Hyacinth*
      by Alphonse Mucha,
      1911)
who lives in a world
built from stars, lilies, irises.
The thrust of my chest
is exaggerated;
my head is raised
like an empress's.

Benjamin keeps his laughter
bottled up,

champagne stifled
by a cork.
It tastes
like the stars.

The museums close
as the sky turns the color of dust
and we dash
over the Legion Bridge
and down the winding stairs
to Střelecký Island.

The thin strip of land
straddles the Vltava
between the two halves of the city.
Careworn oaks
shield Benjamin and me.
There are so many picnic blankets
beneath our feet
we have to dance around them.

Giant swans drift,
unhurried,
across the glass-still water of the river.
But they aren't real swans—
they're paddleboats,
their elegant bodies
only made of plastic.
Yet I can't stop watching them.

A boy
leans over
the edge of a swan boat,
splashing the girl beside him.
She shrieks in false outrage.
Their laughter is a song
that makes my heart ache.

These are the things
I won't ever be able to do with Benjamin.
It shouldn't hurt.
                    (But it does.)

My face begins to glow;
it must look even brighter
than the fairy lights
strung from the rafters
of Aunt Žofie's kitchen.
You must think
these boats are so stupid.
It's not like they're real swans,
I mumble to Benjamin.

The blue-eyed boy wraps his arms
around his knees;
he's never looked so young.
I like them.
They look like they could fly away,

taking their passengers
to a wintry place
white as their feathers.
Maybe we could
go with them,
together.

I have to change the subject,
otherwise I'm going to confess
the only thing
I don't want Benjamin to know.
      (Yet.)
You know Yiddish, don't you?
My mom doesn't speak it,
but it's important to so many Jews.
Teach me a word.
Teach me everything
about the way
the world used to be.

Mishpachah—
means family.
Gute neshome—
a good soul.
Emmis—
the truth.
Benjamin speaks slowly,
as if he's pulling the words

from somewhere
deep inside himself, a place
    (half-forgotten or maybe
    locked away)
he hasn't ventured into
for years.
Now you go, Ilana.
Teach me something new—
something
in Spanish.

The words and phrases
I give him
mean the most
to me, to my mother,
maybe even to those
who came before us.
Acere—
a friend.
El gao—
home.
Arriba de la bola—
to be the greatest.

Tell me, I say again.
Tell me about who
you used to be.

(This game is dangerous.
The more I know about Benjamin,
the closer to him
I want to be.

I tell myself he's dust;
I shouldn't want to be around him
the way I do.
But it doesn't work,
even though the wind
could steal Benjamin from me
whenever it chooses.)

Roses burst
in violet clusters
　　　(the shade
　　　of all things hidden)
on both of Benjamin's wrists.
He smiles, adrift in a memory
that flows from his lips
more smoothly than before.
My father used to force me out of bed
before the sun was even up
to go to heder.
I didn't mind it.
I liked how quiet the streets were
when I walked alongside my friends.
I thought I was seeing the world

the way it was meant to be seen,
without anything in the way.
Do you go to heder, Ilana?

Yes and no.
Mom makes me go to Hebrew class
on Sundays.
I used to pretend to hate it.
I thought that's what you had to do
when you were thirteen, fourteen, fifteen.
But I didn't.
I still don't.

Chapter Twenty-Four

Pearl appears beside us,
sucking her thumb.
Chocolate is smeared
        (impossibly—
        but I've given up
        trying to explain
        magic,
        even to myself)
on her front teeth.

This is the first time
I've seen her and Benjamin
side by side.
I pull in a sharp breath,
startled
by the difference between them.
Pearl is a black-and-white photograph of a girl,
her edges smudged,
her roses pale and fine as mist.
If I touched them,
would they crumble?
Would *she*?

Pearl points
at the sun's reflection in the river;
it is red as a wound.
You have to come home, Benjamin—
it's almost dark!
Onkel Wassermann'll be worried
if we don't get back.

I ask:
Could I come with you?
I'd like to see your house.

Soon, Benjamin says.
But his promise feels brittle,
an ash vow.
I can't say *why* either.

Pearl and the blue-eyed boy
leave without looking back,
the girl-child
swinging her arms in time
with her whistling,
Benjamin's skin weeping
rose petals that darken
with each step he takes.

I shouldn't follow them to Old Town.
It's rude, like peeking through a curtain
at what I'm not meant to see.

But if I knew
what Benjamin was keeping from me,
I might
be able to help him
the way
he's helped me.

My shadow sneaks behind me
as I chase the ghosts,
      quiet
        as a cat.
I run
on the tips of my toes,
trying to mimic it.

It's not difficult to follow the dead.
All I have to do is track the shivers,
the sudden
stops
the living make
whenever Benjamin
and Pearl
pass through them.

As always, the black house is waiting
and so is its owner.
Wassermann isn't a large man,
yet he takes up the entire doorway.
That's just how magic is.
It expands to fill
the space around it.

I hide
behind
the nearest building,
letting the red bricks
conceal my pink cheeks
and the tangle
of my dark hair.

> (I wish these walls
> could tell me
> everything they've seen,
> everything I've *missed*.)

The sunset refuses to touch
Wassermann's black house.
Its wood paneling doesn't shine;
its windows don't gleam.
It's outside of time,
like everything extraordinary.

Wassermann catches Pearl
in his arms,
fitting her against
the bony notch of his hip.

She laughs
(at first)
as he bounces her up
and down.
But the longer he does,
the jerkier the movements become,
the more her gaze is like Benjamin's—
rabbit-like,
afraid of what might happen next.

Benjamin keeps his blue eyes
on the cobblestones,
using the toe of his shoe
          (a hundred years old and counting)
to sketch designs in the dirt.

I can't tell if he is talking
or if Wassermann
is talking *over* him.
He looks too small,
too young,
too muted
to be the boy
I sat with by the water.
          (But I know
          they are one
          and the same.)

Finally, Benjamin marches inside,
a tin soldier
someone has wound up
and set
into motion.

I stay where I am for a long time,
my thoughts howling,
my heart frozen, like the winter
that never really arrives
in Miami.

I *did* see something
I wasn't supposed to.

But I don't know
what it means.

When I was thirteen,
my parents and I
drove to Disney World,
fleeing a hurricane.

The magic there
was packaged,
perfectly choreographed,
frothy as the carbonated drinks
that crackled on my tongue.
It didn't creep
through the cracks
and secret spaces of the world,
like moss growing
between broken slabs of concrete.
That kind of magic
didn't ask for blood
or tears.
It simply *was*.

So when the hurricane
struck Orlando
instead of Miami,
I wasn't sad to be denied
Disney's plastic wonder.
I sat by the light of a tea candle,
listening to the rain
scratch at our windows,

a beast
asking to be let in.

Aunt Žofie
told me the truth
my first morning at Rose Cottage—
real magic
won't ever be safe.
That means it isn't
what most people look for.

But it's the only type of magic
I can believe in.

Rose Cottage is still empty
by the time I return.
The shadows that spring,

        leap,

   dance
in its corners are playful
and light-footed.

I creep
into my aunt's studio,
retrieving the black violin.
My best chance to make sense of things
is with a song.

I float
so far from here, from *now*,
thanks to the passacaglia
stirring
on the strings of the violin
that I almost miss
the witch-wail of the front door
as it announces
Aunt Žofie's arrival.

I stop playing
       (just in time)
and hide the violin again.
But resentment
simmers inside me.

I shouldn't have to stop at all.

There are no Shabbat candles
in my aunt's cupboards.
I have to make do
with a mismatched set:
one made of beeswax,
the other white as the snow
I've never seen.

I light both
beside the window

as night settles
over Aunt Žofie's garden.

I move my hands
over the candles,
sweeping up their brilliance,
drawing it into me.

> *Baruch ata Adonai,*
> *Eloheinu Melech ha-olam,*
> *asher kidshanu b'mitzvotav*
> *v'zivanu l'hadlik ner shel Shabbat.*

Aunt Žofie watches me quietly.
She may not understand,
but she knows
how important the ritual is to me—
  like the cemetery,
  like my ghost,
  like the music I can't admit
  I'm still playing.

I hope that in the black house,
Pearl is lighting candles herself,
and Benjamin
is helping her
welcome the Shabbat queen.

Chapter Twenty-Five

Benjamin must not know
I followed him and Pearl through Old Town;
he is all smiles
when he greets me in the cemetery
on Sunday.

I want you to meet the boys
I've known for so long
they're almost my little brothers, Benjamin says.
Will you let me take you to them?

I laugh my yes.
What was I so afraid of on Friday?
Benjamin must be happy
in the black house,
even if his existence
isn't perfect,
even if Wassermann is stricter
than he might like.
My parents are the same way.

I let Benjamin lead me
through the garden, hungry

(always hungry now)

to be part of his
        (after)
life.

I fly down the road,
the concrete
sizzling, popping
under the wheels of Aunt's Žofie's
mint-colored bicycle.
The black violin is in the basket;
its strings
try to sing
as it rattles in its case.

Benjamin sits behind me
and for the first time,
I can *feel*
        his wrist digging into my hip,
        the swell of his belly
        fitting into the small of my back.

Am I imagining things?
Have I remembered Benjamin to life?
Or has the blue-eyed boy himself
recalled:
        how to be made of breath and bone,
        how to fit an arm around a girl's waist,
        how to be part of a city

that moved on without him
in the summer heat?

I don't know.
But maybe one day,
Benjamin will fool time itself
and it will allow him
back into Prague,
solid enough
for me to wrap myself
around properly.

Steadying my heartbeat,
I follow the map
Benjamin murmurs
in my ear.
We pass under Charles Bridge
and into another park
beside the river.

Two
(dead)
children stand
in the shadow of a tree
so old
it could be the same one
Queen Libuše sat beneath
when she met her husband,

the plowman
who would be king.

I wave
at Benjamin's near-brothers.
Their eyes
      (deep and brown
      as spring earth)
widen.

These children are much younger
than the boy I can
      (nearly)
call mine;
they're only nine
      or ten.
They're dimmer than Benjamin is,
winking in and out
like stars
as I stare at them.

But their clothes
remind me of his:
crisp white shirts,
dark trousers,
their socks rumpled,
their kipot lopsided.

Did the twins
plan every wrinkle
in their slacks to match?
Did they intend to be
such perfect mirrors?
Or were they born this way
in the twentieth century's early days?

In Miami,
I would have been so jealous of these boys.
I'd never had a friend so close
that I couldn't tell
where he began
and I ended
until Benjamin.

Maybe he and I
are supposed to be twins.
Maybe we were,
in some other life.
Maybe our souls
were hidden away
inside birds
or fauns
to keep us safe
from a witch,
a viper,
a plague.

Maybe we walked
the streets of a different city,
in another time and place,
together,
just like we do now.

I'm Lior, says the first boy.
And my brother
is Issur.

Lior bounces,
his soul
a shiny red balloon
ready to float away
into the July skyline.
But the roses growing
under his rumpled collar
are in a sad state,
just like Pearl's.
They contain
only a hint of sunshine yellow.
Onkel Wassermann
told us all about you.

He says
you're going to be our friend.
Is that true?
Issur's words have gravity,

a heaviness
that his twin's do not.

Of course, I promise.
Any friend of Benjamin's
is a friend of mine.

Issur and Lior
form the ends
of each other's sentences,
a ring of never-ending boyhood
and all the light that comes with it.

But girlhood is different.
It comes with pain—
the bite of my ruby slippers
against the backs of my ankles,
the hard snap of rhinestone nails
on the summit of my kneecap,
my scalp prickling
as I bleached my hair
when I was fourteen.

Pain like that turns pleasant;
you start thinking of it
as an accomplishment.
It always goes along
with prettiness.

And we've been told:
nothing is better than that.

The twins race back
and forth
across the park.
Their *payos* strike their cheeks
as they wave imaginary swords
at an equally imaginary enemy.

Boys in Miami
wear their hair the same way.
The twins
wouldn't be out of place
in this day and age,
if only they could step
out of the history
forming a gulf between them
and the living.

Be a monster, Benjamin!
the twins yell.
Be a monster for us!

You're about to see me
embarrass myself, Ilana.
Benjamin laughs,
pushing his hair back

in time
with a gust of wind from the river.
Having little brothers
means relearning
how to play pretend.
Every time we come
to the park,
I become someone different,
just
for them—
a beast or a knight,
a villain or a hero.

Which monster
should I be?
Benjamin asks
the two boys.
A golem
run wild?
You'll have to scrub
the Name off me.
A čert?
Be clever and I might
let your souls get away.

A story I read
in one of Aunt Žofie's books
unspools
on my tongue.

You could be
a vodník.
A river spirit.

The three ghosts
shudder
to a stop,
marionettes whose strings
I've cut
with only a single word.

A single *monster.*

But why?

Then Benjamin speaks
like I never did.
I'll be a golem!
A friend turned enemy.
Come!
Let's play.

I can't join their game
without looking unhinged.
There's only so much laughter
I can share
with invisible boys
before someone questions it.

I sit on the nearest bench,
grateful for a moment alone—
which means that someone
has to come
and interrupt it.

Rudolf Wassermann
takes a seat beside me.
He may not have a shadow,
but he's become mine.
He wears tacky sunglasses today,
dark as his violin.
The left lens is scratched—
another imperfection
I can add
to the list of his flaws.

An old woman passes us,
stirring
the hem of Wassermann's coat.
She bumps against his knee, saying:
> *Prominňte*
as she departs.

The man with no shadow
answers my question
before I can fully shape it.
I can be seen if I want to be.

Didn't Benjamin tell you?
I'm not dead,
not buried in the cemetery
alongside
Pearl,
Benjamin,
the twins.

I ask him:
Then what are you?

Something
from a much older world.
Wassermann props his right ankle
on his left knee, a song
      (Piano Quartet No. 3
      in C minor, Op. 60,
      "Werther Quartet,"
      Brahms)
already on his lips.

I'm not a song;
I'm not made of half-steps and downbeats.
So why do I get the feeling
that if anyone could make me one,
it's Wassermann?

      (It would be so much easier
      than being a girl.)

Benjamin takes off his cap,
shuffling over to the two of us.
His head is open to the sky.
I've never seen him
anything less than pious
before now.

Sir, he says to Wassermann,
in a tone that actually implies:
Your Excellency.

Wassermann nods,
an emperor
acknowledging his subject,
and Benjamin sits
next to me.

With a magician's sleight of hand
and a twist of his long fingers,
Wassermann passes me
a chocolate square.

It glues my mouth closed
when I shove it
between my painted lips.
But my head is throbbing
and the sweetness is a buffer

against the hum of pain
brought on by the heat.

(Or something else.)

Why don't you join us
at the opera tomorrow, Ilana?
Wassermann tips his sunglasses down.
He carries the oncoming night
in his eyes.
I always have tickets.
Why, I even have my own box!
I often take the children with me—
you of all people know
how important music is.

His smile is unlovely as ever.
But I haven't been to the opera before;
it always seemed
dazzling, jeweled,
important.

I never thought of myself
as important
before the cemetery,
before the black violin,
before Benjamin,
before *this.*

I was the sum of my parents' dreams
and I rarely managed
to make any of them
        come true.

Benjamin crushes his hand
in mine,
setting fireworks off
under my skin.
I can feel his fingers
pressing
up
against my own.
His touch is more
than a daydream;
it's no fantasy
brought on by the heat.

Please come, Benjamin says.
You'll enjoy it.

In my mind,
I'm already crafting excuses
        like poems
to go out tomorrow night.
Aunt Žofie preaches
love, passion,
the more vibrant things in life.

Maybe she wouldn't mind
if I went on a date with a boy.

She doesn't need to know
that the boy
in question
is dead.

Have you learned to play
"The Last Rose of Summer"?
I'd love
to hear your progress,
says Wassermann.

I nod,
taking the violin
from the bicycle's basket.

The man with no shadow
rises,
adjusting the slant of my shoulders,
the position of the bow.
Breathe, he whispers.
You
are still
alive.

Right now,
the only things that matter
in this broken world are:
the music I play,
the shining eyes of the dead boys,
and the creature
they call their uncle.

As they watch me
make my own magic,
I don't think
I've ever been happier.

The light eventually escapes us
and I have to say goodbye.
But before I do,
Benjamin offers
to take me back to Rose Hill.

Wassermann frowns at him.
Come home soon, he instructs.

Benjamin nods.
But he's barely paying attention.
He can't keep his eyes
off
of
me.

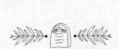

Chapter Twenty-Six

As we reach the guard tower
at the beginning of Charles Bridge,
the first star
rises over our heads.

Benjamin and I
       (the ghost and the girl)
            pause,
taking in the full expanse of sky,
a dark sea
we try to navigate.

I haven't seen the stars
in so long, Benjamin breathes.
      (Or as close to it
      as he can.)
I've felt so different
since you've come to Prague.
I feel like I'm more than I was,
more than I've been
since I was alive.

You were always more, I say.
You just had to remember it.

I don't know how to kiss Benjamin.
Will my lips pass
through his,
will I be able to feel his mouth
against mine,
will he be able
to feel anything at all?

But I can't wait
any longer.
I love you, Benjamin.

Benjamin stumbles over
the words that come next—
he's speaking
English, German,
Czech, Yiddish,
all at once.
But I can still understand him.

Ilana, I'm dead.
I can't give you anything.
He turns out
his pockets.
They are as empty
as the eyes of the statues
who watch us
from their pedestals.

I don't care that you're dead, I say.
You're here, with me.
You can read my heart
like it's yours—
that's all that matters.

The boy bites his lip,
then lowers his head
as if he's praying.

       (He might be.
       I know I am.)

Benjamin's kiss travels
all
the
way
down
my spine.

The feeling of it grows
between my ribs
like his roses—
sharp, tender, perfect.

His tongue
speaks a secret language
to mine,

and his hands
brush my shoulder blades,
making me feel
as if I have wings.

The kiss lasts
for his lifetime
and my unfolding one.
It reaches lives
we haven't lived yet,
and all the ones
we've forgotten.

When we come back
down to earth,
to Prague,
to *now*,
I feel like
someone new.

A flower bursts
from Benjamin's cheek,
its scarlet petals
shattering
the deep purple of nightfall.
Was that ...
Was that all right?

Kiss me again
and I'll tell you.

What does it mean
for me to have kissed Benjamin
and not have him crumble
to dust
beneath my lips?

How much strange magic
is waiting for me
       (in Prague,
       in Miami,
       in the world)
if it's possible
for a ghost's hands
to feel as strong
as those of any other boy?

I stumble into Rose Cottage,
where Aunt Žofie
is preparing dinner.

I need to talk to *someone*
who has already fallen in love,
who might know
what happens next.
And I can't call my mother.

She'd be furious
I was spending time with a boy,
no matter how kind he is.

I ask Aunt Žofie:
How old were you
when you had
your first kiss?

My aunt
stops
stirring the *česnečka*,
the garlic soup.
This is our evening ritual;
she cooks
while I daydream
on a chair
she painted sunflowers on.
But usually, she is the one
who starts a conversation—
not me.

I was about your age.
Maybe a little younger, she says.
It was not long
after your dad left.
I felt
like your father
had abandoned me.

*I was desperate to shake off
my sadness, my rage,
my confusion.*

*I'd go to secret parties
where everyone
did forbidden Western things.
We wore jeans
and listened to David Bowie,
Freddie Mercury,
singers
who were more like stories
come to life
than men.*

*I didn't know the name
of the boy
        (lamppost skinny)
who kissed me,
who I kissed back.
But when we danced together,
I thought I could fly
to Paris, London,
some other land
where I could be free.*

I trace the golden outline
of the sunflowers on my chair.

So you didn't love him?
This boy you kissed?

You don't need to be in love
to kiss someone.
But it helps.
Aunt Žofie's smile
is more smirk
when she asks:
And you?

I don't blush;
at sixteen,
I bet Aunt Žofie
had kissed dozens of boys.
And by now?
She's probably seen
      (and heard
        and done)
it all.
My first kiss
was at a party last year—
just like you.
I didn't love that boy, though.
He was too rough
and he didn't love me either.

I'll take Benjamin's soft kiss
over the one that felt like a forest fire,
the one that tried to
      burn
      me
      up,
remake me
into a girl
I've never been,
all so a boy
wouldn't go to bed
hungry for more.

Chapter Twenty-Seven

The opera ticket arrives
under the cloak of daylight,
the way the black violin did.

I'm dreaming of excuses
to go out tonight
when I finally see the note
Aunt Žofie left behind.
It peeks out from under a cup
of fresh hibiscus tea.
Call your father.

I groan.
Her instructions are so much less magical
than anything else
in my life.

I recharge my phone,
but I barely glance
at the desperate pleas
>   *(Text me!*
>   *Email me!*
>   *Where are you?*
>   *You haven't posted anything*
>   *in weeks!)*
Martina and Sarah left behind.

What can I say to them?
What would we even talk about?
I can't go back to being
the girl I was
on the beach.
She's as lost to time
as Benjamin is.

I bounce from foot to foot
as I wait for Dad
to pick up.

Hello, Ilana.
Dad's greeting
is a sigh.
I heard
you've been
running around
with some boy
and playing music
instead of studying.

There's no question
how Dad knows—
Aunt Žofie
must have seen Benjamin,
heard me playing
the black violin.
But why
would she tell my father?
I thought
she was on *my* side!

Your mother and I
expected you to be
more responsible than this, *Ilana!*
I didn't want to send you
to Prague and now
I can see I was right.
Now is the time to concentrate

on important things—
your grades,
getting into a good university,
planning for your future.

The course
you're on
will make your life small.
It will be a life of poverty,
full of struggle,
and you will have to fight
for everything,
the way
your mom and I
had to.
But if you choose wisely now,
you won't *need to.*

Dad's words are like stones
slipped into my pocket,
weighing me down.
A month ago,
two months ago,
I would have bowed my head,
and promised to bury
my dreams.

I don't now.

With music in it,
my life won't ever be small,
it won't ever be poor.
And the boy
I've been seeing
understands who I am.
Why can't you trust
the choices I make?
My future
isn't your past.

I try to sound fierce,
like a girl who loves ghosts
more than she fears them,
like a girl who has dangerous secrets.
But my voice doesn't quite rally
in my defense.

Ilana—

I won't listen anymore,
because I know
Dad won't listen to *me*.

I hang up the phone,
tossing it onto the counter.

There's as much power
in ending a conversation
as there is in starting one.

My blood buzzes.
If I tried to pour my anger
into a song,
the black violin
might burst into flames.

I can't keep
myself hidden
any longer.

But my parents will only be happy
if I'm an unfinished symphony.
And my aunt
is (apparently) no different.

I tear
through Aunt Žofie's closet,
searching for a gown,
Cinderella gone mad.

I arm myself with:
high-heeled shoes
lipstick red as blood,
rings as hard
as my diamond heart.

I take the opera ticket;
I leave no note.

My ill-gotten shoes
cut into my feet.
But it feels good
to hurt.

Interlude III:
Wassermann

You must understand:
if the Germans
had not invaded Prague
like a mischief of rats,
I never
would have gone hungry
again.

But the Nazis
took the children
far from the hill of roses
by train,
by truck,
by bullet,
and buried them
in icy fields
far from the Vltava.

They stole from me
as they stole
artwork,
candlesticks,
books whose pages
crumbled like borders
under siege
from the museums
and the homes
of anyone they deemed
an *Untermensch*—
less than human.

(As if humanity
was anything to be proud of!)

The last child
I took
was Pearl
and I have already eaten
most of her.

But there will be
new children now,
thanks to Ilana.

And I am
so
looking
forward
to meeting them.

Third Movement:
The Lost Children

Chapter Twenty-Eight

The art center in Miami is modern.
Its glass walls
reflect a person's own ideas
back at them.
Sarah, Martina, and I
left performances
dreaming
about what it would be like
to stand onstage,
listening to the roar of strings
and the applause that followed.

But Prague's State Opera house
leaves no room
for anyone's thoughts.

It's too crowded with memories,
men in suits
      (soft as Benjamin's kiss)
and women wearing jewels
in shades of moonlight.

I'm here
because of music.
I'm here
because of Benjamin.
I'm here
because a man with no shadow
cares more about
what I want
than my own family does.

Seeing the dead kids and Wassermann
lined up beside the grand staircase
makes me sway in my
      (stolen)
heels.

Lior and Issur have matching suits;
yellow roses
      (dim as candlelight)
crawl down their arms.
Pearl wears
a white confection of a gown,
all frothing tulle.

It matches
her wintry flowers
and the streaks of white
in her otherwise dark hair.
      (Were they there before?
      It's hard to tell.)
And in front of the children
is Benjamin.

He looks so tall,
a solid oak tree
of a boy.
In his suit,
he could be royalty,
crowned
by the shimmering lights.
I want to tell him this,
but I can't uncage my voice.

Benjamin smiles,
as if I am the only girl in the world,
sunflower radiant.
Hello, Ilana.

The five of us
take our seats
high above the rest of the audience.
The lights go down;

the strings hum in the orchestra pit,
preparing to usher me
into a story.

In the rising tide of darkness,
Benjamin takes my hand.
I hold on to his
just as tightly.
He is so *real*,
so much more
than a twentieth-century shadow
casting itself
over the present.

And I am a princess, loved
by a prince.
I am a girl, discovered
by a wizard.

I am finally
where I *belong*.

The music of the opera
leaves me feeling drunk.
When the first act ends,
my head
is full to bursting.

During intermission,
I guide Benjamin
into the opera house's shadows
and kiss him
again and again.

I've found sanctuary
inside a boy,
a song,
a city,
a moment.
I hope
Benjamin has found sanctuary
inside me too.

The houselights flicker,
signaling that the performance
will soon begin again.
Benjamin and I can't stay here,
cloaked in music
and time
we don't have.

But I like to imagine
we could.

When the opera is over,
and the silence crowds around us,

Wassermann bows his head.
His mouth hangs above me,
a sickle moon
on the horizon.

I want you
to stay in Prague.
I want you
to live with us.
His accent thickens
with every word.
I could teach you
true magic.
And you could
play music, now
and forever.
I can give you
the gift that I carry—
life eternal.

The question that unfolds
on my tongue
is the only one
that matters.
Why me?

Rudolf Wassermann's smile
is endless as the sea.

Because you're talented.
Because you see us
as we are.
Because Benjamin
loves you.

What happens
to the families of the girls
who step through enchanted doorways
and never return?

The books I read when I was little
never gave an answer.
But as I've learned,
just because someone disappears
doesn't mean
they're forgotten
by everyone.
Grief fills
the holes in the world
they leave behind.

What about my parents?
My aunt?
My friends back home?
What will they think?

Wassermann shakes his head.

They don't need you, Ilana.
They don't appreciate you.
But Benjamin,
the other children,
and I...
We want you
to be part of our family.
We know
how very special
you really are.

I walk,
stunned,
into the velvet night.

Benjamin trails after me,
a falling star
who has finally reached earth.
He asked you, didn't he?
Wassermann asked you
to join us.

Yes.
The word
rolls off my tongue
so easily.
I almost want to run inside
and offer the same one to Wassermann

right here and now.
I'll never be
what my parents hoped for.
I'm too much myself.

Please, don't.
Benjamin's voice
is gentle as twilight.
But his eyes beg me
to stop dreaming
and start listening.

Ilana, I need
to tell you
the truth.
Wassermann's magic
stopped me
from doing it
so many times before.
But thanks to you,
I remember who I am.
Thanks to you,
I'm finally strong enough
to push back
against Wassermann.

Here is the truth
my blue-eyed boy imparts

under the eye of the moon:
Wassermann is the monster
you named
in the game
the twins and I played—
the vodník.

He is always hungry, Ilana.
He's trapped us in Prague.
And he'll trap you here too.

I love you, **says Benjamin.**

I've wanted to hear him tell me so
since we first kissed.
But not
      like
          this.

I choke
on my response.
Words fill my throat,
a row of poison apple seeds.
I don't understand.

Benjamin shakes me.
I love you
and that's why

I'm telling you this.
If you stay with us,
you'll become like Wassermann,
always starving
for more,
willing to do anything
to get it.

Please, Benjamin begs.
Even if it means
we have to say goodbye,
you don't deserve
Wassermann's fate.
The world can be cruel,
I know.
Don't be cruel
alongside it.
Don't become like him—
like me.

I pick up my skirts
and flee,
kicking my bloody shoes aside
once I reach the river.
They tumble down the bank;
the black water accepts
my heartbreak.

I'm diving even deeper
into the tale
I'm trying to escape from.

But I have to get away.
I trusted Benjamin;
I trusted Wassermann.
I trusted that the music
wouldn't lead me astray.

But I've wandered
far from the path,
    the safety
        offered by an orderly life
and realized
I've been
in the company of monsters
all this time.

My aunt's anger
lights up the threshold of Rose Cottage.

We need to talk—
four ominous words.
But for once,
they don't make
my heart quake.

Nothing Aunt Žofie says
can be worse
than what I've already heard.

Chapter Twenty-Nine

At this hour,
my aunt's studio
looks like a witch's lair.
Every paintbrush is a wand;
every canvas a spell book.

I'm bracing for the truth—
but knowing
is better than *not*.
I say:
Tell me
what's really
going on.

Aunt Žofie turns from the shadows.
I told your father
you were playing music again
and spending time
with the dead boy
because I wanted you
to give them both up.

I'm sorry
for betraying you,
but both the ghost
and the black violin
belong to a monster.

His name
is Rudolf Wassermann,
I say.
Have you met him?

Aunt Žofie
shakes her head.
I haven't.
But I've heard of him.
The creature's real name
is the vodník,
the river man.

My heart skips.
The creature
in one of her books
is the reality
that's been in front of me
the entire summer.

The vodník **wasn't born here;**
no part of our river

runs through his veins.
He came from Germany.
My aunt's look is darker
than the midnight hour
closing in on us.
My grandmother, Babička, told me
he traps the souls of children
in a teapot.
Without those souls,
he'd become mortal,
doomed to ashes
and dust.

Babička warned me:
"To be around the dead
is to call the vodník
from the water."
I only half-believed her.
Still, I turned away
from ghosts and anything else
that had already given in
to decay.
I see now that I was right.
I never should have let you
climb Rose Hill.

I still don't understand, I say.
If Wassermann is the vodník,

why does he care about me?
I'm not a ghost—
I'm alive.

                                     Even if the boy I love
                                     isn't
                                     and never will be
                                     again.

Why do you think the thirteenth fairy
cursed Briar Rose?
Why do you think Snow White's stepmother
asked for her daughter's heart?
Aunt Žofie shrugs.
Some creatures are empty—
they'll do anything
to be filled up,
even for an instant.

For the vodník *to show*
such interest in you,
he must believe
you can give him
whatever it is
he needs.

Aunt Žofie clasps my hands
in hers.

You must stay away
from the river man, Ilana.
I can't lose you.
And neither
can your parents.
They are strict, yes,
but I know
everything they say and do
springs from love.
Turn away from the magic
before it's too late.
Please.

I want to promise her
I'll do just that.
But all I can think of
is Benjamin.

Maybe sixteen is a curse,
a time when everyone is stuck
between being a child
and being something else.

Maybe that's why
we find our ghosts then.
Maybe that's why
monsters like Wassermann
find *us*.

Sleep escapes me that night
and Aunt Žofie refuses to let me leave
Rose Cottage
when I finally stumble
out of bed.

The hours pass,
syrupy, school-day slow.
I catch myself
looking
over my shoulder,
waiting
for the gentle hand
of a dead boy
to settle on my skin.

But Benjamin doesn't come for me.

Dad texts me three times;
Mom calls me twice.
I ignore them both,
not out of spite
but because I don't know
how to respond.
Their messages feel so distant,
missives
from the other side of the galaxy.

How can I think about the future
when the past
      (Wassermann the eternal,
      his house of ghosts,
      the graveyard he took them from)
won't let me go?

At dusk,
I sneak out to the cemetery
and wait
beside Benjamin's grave.

It's not long
before the air around me shivers
and the blue-eyed boy arrives.
But for once,
I don't smile at him.

I want the full truth, I say.
I want to know
everything you know.
You owe me that much.

Benjamin draws a breath.
You've helped me become stronger
than I ever was before.
I can show you now.

He doesn't wait
for my permission to put his
    (cold)
hands
on my face.

My world falls away,
and is replaced
by his.

Chapter Thirty

In the beginning,
there was a boat
on the Vltava
    when the war
        to end all wars
            had ended
and a boy
    named Benjamin
who fell
into the river.

The water filled his lungs.
He believed, then,
that he was going to die.

He didn't realize
the dying would come later.

The fever brought on
by the river water
came suddenly,
an invasion
no one
had prepared for.

The defenses
mounted by doctors,
tears,
prayers
failed.
Benjamin's mother wept
in Czech.
His father cursed
in German.

> (*The Germans
> have a word
> for everything,*
> Benjamin says grimly.)

His parents begged God
in Yiddish,
Hebrew.

His sister bargained
in the language of silence.
And Benjamin thrashed
in his bed,
August fire
raging inside him.

> *(When a phoenix burns,*
> *it rises from the ashes.*
> *But I was a boy,*
> *not a bird.*
> *And when I burned,*
> *there was nothing*
> *left of me.)*

When Benjamin's soul
left his body,
he hovered
near his family,
a dream,
unfulfilled.

I'm fine! he cried.
It doesn't hurt anymore!
Please, don't be sad!

But they sobbed
and wailed, unable to hear him.

His father ripped
the collar of his shirt,
his shoulders trembling.
His mother and sister
held each other
as they longed to hold Benjamin
one last time.

Benjamin's family
carried the plain pine box
his body lay inside
up Rose Hill
the very next day.

And Benjamin followed behind,
no longer struggling
for breath.

> *(It was the only good thing
> about being dead.)*

They prayed,
lowered the coffin

                                        (his coffin)

into the ground,
shoveled the dirt
over him.

Benjamin's family
had seen him into the world;
now they helped usher him out of it.

But he
did not leave.

> (Benjamin whispers:
> *I didn't go back*
> *to my family's house.*
> *I should have.*
> *But I was a coward.*
> *I didn't want to see*
> *how much pain*
> *they were in.*)

It wasn't until Benjamin's parents
laid his headstone
a month later
that Wassermann
found him.

> (Regret
> darkens
> Benjamin's eyes
> and his roses
> to midnight blue.
> *People believe that you'll recognize*

the monsters in your life
the first time you meet them.
They don't realize
the greatest of monsters
always appear
as the best of friends.)

The man without a shadow arrived
whistling
and waltzing
around the headstones
to the music
in his head.
He was mad for it, as ever.

(*Wassermann confused me,*
Benjamin says.
With a song in his mouth
and sour cherry jam
on his left hand,
            red as blood,
I knew he couldn't be a Jew.
You shouldn't sing
or eat
in a cemetery.
We never want our dead
to long
for what they cannot have.)

Why, hello there, young man!
Wassermann said.
His white leather coat
billowed outward,
a stolen piece of winter sky.

Benjamin stared.
I...I didn't think
anyone
could see me.
Are you dead too?

Wassermann shook his head.
I'm not dead.
I'm just different.

Benjamin had always liked things
that were different.
I suppose I'm different too,
he said,
thinking of
six-toed cats
and gray cygnets.

Wassermann wrung
his hands together,
as if he were praying
for the departed Benjamin.

It's always a tragedy
when a child dies
as young as you are.

His gaze fell
on the dead boy's headstone.
Tell me, Benjamin,
why haven't you moved on
to ... wherever?

I can't, said Benjamin.
My sister is here.
My family is here.
I can't leave
until they do.

Wassermann's eyes glinted
when he suggested:
Why not stay with me
until it's time to be reunited
with your family?
I have a lovely house
and like you, it is
extraordinary.

Benjamin gasped.
You would let me
stay with you?
But you just met me!

You're alone, said Wassermann.
So am I.

> (And for all his lies,
> I knew
> in that moment
> Wassermann was as lonely
> as a well without water.)

Will you come with me, Benjamin?
Will you come home?

I'm powerless
to stop the boy I love
from taking Wassermann's hand
and walking
into the night
alongside him.

> (*It wasn't until*
> *I entered the black house*
> *that I realized*
> *what I'd done.*
> *I belonged to him,* says Benjamin.
> *He held my soul*
> *then and now*
> *and for all time.*)

The boogeyman
exists in every country.
Aunt Žofie and Benjamin
name him
the *vodník*;
Mom called him
el Viejo del Saco—
the sack man,
who stuffed wayward children
into his bag and carried them
far from the light.
The song is the same;
it's only played
in a slightly different key.

Chapter Thirty-One

I flick my tears away.
They feel so pointless;
I can't make a sword from them,
or an arrow
that might crack
Wassermann's heart
in two.

Benjamin pulls his knees
up to his chin.
The vodník
stole the dead
the same way
every time.
He would go to the cemetery
after a child
passed away
and lure us back to his house.
Pearl was the last one
he caught.

Strawberry girl, I whisper.
As if I can give her
a name that Wassermann
doesn't own.

In 1941,
the Germans smashed
the cemetery
with hammers,
bullets,
their own strong
and hateful fists.

I wept
when I returned

and saw the broken pieces,
the granite lions,
the cracked stone vineyards.
I couldn't understand
why they hated us
so much.

Wassermann was furious
about the cemetery.
His hunting ground was gone.
But one last child
was buried here
before it was destroyed:
Pearl.
She starved,
as so many did
after the Nazis invaded.

And when she awoke here,
Wassermann was waiting,
with a truffle
in his hand.

Benjamin swallows.
Now there's a hole
where most of Pearl's memories
should be.

It won't be long
before she only remembers
loving
and being loved
by Wassermann.
He took everything else
away from her.

I can't think of anything worse
for the strawberry girl.
The Germans
stole her life,
but Wassermann stole
her childhood.

The truth of everything
fills my mouth
like bile.
Benjamin!
Your memories ...
Wassermann's eating them,
isn't he?
He's eating your souls.

Yes, Benjamin murmurs.
The dead are made of memories—
when those are gone,
we disappear.

The Ghosts of Rose Hill

There used to be so many more ghosts
in the black house.
But Wassermann ate us,
one by one.
Now only Pearl and I
and the twins
remain.

Why can't the others
see
        (and *feel*)
how threadbare
they've become,
how their colors
are bleeding out,
how their roses wilt
a little more
each day?

I don't need to ask
my question aloud;
Benjamin answers it anyway.
Lior, Issur, and Pearl
believe Wassermann loves them,
because they *love* him.
All *the children he ate did.*
And when you're dead,
what else
is there to love?

I fall backward.
The grass feels too soft
for this conversation.
What can I do?

Nothing, says Benjamin.
I only told you
because I wanted you
to know the truth.

I take his hands.
Please, Benjamin.
I can help you!
Let me try to find a way.

Benjamin
pulls back.
Go home, Ilana.
Go home and forget
any of this
ever happened.

The light in my aunt's room
snaps on,
its glow
lullaby soft.

It's tempting
to stop listening to Benjamin,
to creep back inside
and hide from the dark things
ruling Prague.
I could return to the future—
my future.

But here in the cemetery,
it's impossible
not to think about how
the Nazis stole Jews,
the governments of my parents' youths
stole friends, thoughts, ideas,
poems.

I can't let Wassermann
do the same thing.

The children in the black house
can't leave
unless Wassermann lets them go.
And I don't think
he ever will.

Not unless
someone
makes him.

I say:
You told me
I was a miracle.
I think you're one too, Benjamin.
We're strong together.
We can win
against Wassermann.

Benjamin swallows.
I can see something
begin to glimmer in his eyes.
I know Wassermann
keeps our souls
hidden away in his house,
he says.
I've looked
but never found them.
It's an ancient place
with too many secrets.

My aunt said
he keeps the souls of the dead
in a teapot,
I whisper,
afraid Wassermann might hear me,
even from such a great distance.
If we find it,
if we break it,
you can finally be free!

Free.
Benjamin says the word
as if it's a song
he's never heard before.

But his freedom
will have a price.

I'll lose Benjamin
because I love him,
because he deserves better
than being sixteen
forever.

I curl myself around the space
where Benjamin is
and isn't.
The dewdrops
caught on the leaves above us
imitate the stars.

I want to tell Benjamin:
Hold me,
because soon
you won't be able to.
Hold me,
because I'm about to walk
into the monster's lair

and I'll need to remember
something beautiful.

Somehow,
he knows exactly
what I need.
He folds his arms around me
and I lean into the cold.

Chapter Thirty-Two

The purple night
melts into dawn
and Aunt Žofie tumbles into bed.
I'll have hours
before she'll wake and look for me.

I put the key to Rose Cottage
on a chain around my neck.
It beats
against my collarbone
as I cross Charles Bridge
and run
down the lanes
to where the black house
sits in Old Town, hunched and twisted
like a gargoyle.

I should have left
Aunt Žofie a note.
I should have called
my mother back.

> (I should never have come
> in the first place.)

> But
>   here
>   I
>   am.

I knock,
more than half-hoping
Wassermann won't answer.

I am both lucky and unlucky.
He opens the door with a flourish
and a smile.
Ilana!
How lovely it is
to see you!

I remember the girls
in every Degas painting,
ballerinas

made of a man's
gossamer dreams.
I try to be like them,
peeking up
through my lashes
at Wassermann, demure
as a watercolor.

You were right, I tell him.
About my aunt
and mom and dad.
They don't care about me.
My parents
sent me away to change who I am.
My old friends
don't even bother to talk to me.
And Aunt Žofie's too caught up
in her own life.
None of them
understand me.
But
you
do.

The lies
taste like black licorice,
because some of them
are almost true.

I want to be
around people
who care,
people who want me
to be myself, I say.
Benjamin's my best friend.
I want to stay
beside him
always.

Interlude IV:
Wassermann

This is my very favorite part—
the splendid moment
when a boy
or a girl
comes to me
of their own free will,
hearts splintered
by sorrow,
souls aching
for love denied
or lost.

Centuries of practice
have made an actor of me.
I've gotten so *good*
at arranging tears on my face.
as I listen to the despair
of a child

who has realized
they can never
go home again.

But Ilana is different.
She's more
than just her sadness.
The girl lights up
every room she enters
in the softest hues
of pink and gold.
It blinds me,
but I can't
ever
seem
to look away.

I have to stop myself
from licking my lips.

She is going to be mine
mine
mine.

Chapter Thirty-Three

Wassermann escorts me
to another café.
I'm not allowed
into the black house.
I haven't signed
my soul away.
         (Yet.)

He orders us chocolate cake,
thick slabs of gingerbread,
palačinky dripping
with vanilla cream sauce
on frosted glass plates.

I don't want to take anything
Wassermann gives me,
but I'm too hungry
not to.

In the gloom of the café
Wassermann folds himself up
like a letter tucked away
inside an envelope.
He tells me:

I came from Bavaria,
where they ate their fairy tales.
There was no monster
who could not be turned
into the first course
at dinner,
no extraordinary beast
whose head did not wind up
on a wall.

They wore necklaces of harpy talons
beneath their finely pressed suits.
They bottled the voice of the west wind,
adding it to their morning tea.

The Bavarians tried to empty
the world of wonder—
myself included.
But they failed.

The man with no shadow
breaks off a piece of gingerbread,
sucking on a corner,
needy.
I see my own hunger
        reflected
back at me.

I flex my fingers, wishing
I had something to hold—
a violin bow,
a paintbrush,
the hilt of a sword.
Anything
that would stop me
from feeling
so powerless.

But the only power
I have
is in my lies.

I'm sorry you're in exile, I say.
My family is just a chain
of people who can't
go home again either.

Wassermann crushes his hand on top of mine
in a parody of love.
> (It's very hard
> not to scream.)
It's as if
I were always
meant to find you!
You're a clever girl, Ilana.
I do so appreciate cleverness.

There's never been
a living girl
in my house.
But I'm sure
it will be good
for all of us.
Meet me tomorrow
on Charles Bridge
and I'll take you
to your new home.

If I stayed with him
long enough,
would I force myself to become friends
with Wassermann
in order to survive?

Would I laugh at his jokes
and accept the way
he tweaks the tail of my braid?
Would I play
the black violin
for him
      (and only him)
until my fingers bled?
Would I call him
Uncle, Strýc, Onkel?

There are so many words
for what he could be.
I hope
not to learn any of them.

I am back in bed
before Aunt Žofie wakes.
She checks on me when she does,
and I force my breath
to slow,
mezzo piano.

My aunt would stop me
if she knew
what I was planning.

If you love a person,
you never let them venture
into the dark alone.

To rescue the dead, I need:
more salt than I can hold
in my hands,
more Psalms than I can carry
on my tongue,
more courage than I can lock
in my bones.

What I have:
my own (trembling) heart,
a ghost,
and a black violin.

I remind myself:
    my mother's name means *wolf*.
I remind myself:
    my family always survives
    the ones who hunt them.
I remind myself:
    Prague is as much
    my city
    as it is Wassermann's now.

Chapter Thirty-Four

In the movies,
only one girl is allowed
to survive the monster.

There's something fascinating
about that final girl,
the one who leaves
the haunted house,
the basement,
the cabin in the woods
when all the others
are gone.

They say the final girl
is the last one standing
because she's pure.

But they're wrong.

The final girl survives
because she can be
just as ruthless
as the monster
who wants
to destroy her.

Mom once told me,
if anyone ever tried to snatch me,
I had to fight them
with everything I had.

She pulled my hair back
into a ponytail,
like she was already
preparing me for battle.
*Your legs
are stronger than
your fists.
Yell "Fire!"
It's how someone will know
you're in danger,
because we live
in a world
where "Help!"
is ignored.*

I don't think
she ever believed
I'd *let* myself
be kidnapped by a beast—
     man-shaped
     or otherwise.
But that's exactly
what I'm going to do.

On the morning of my departure,
I take the black violin
and little else.
Nothing Aunt Žofie owns
can help me now.

I lock the door to Rose Cottage
for what might be
the last time
and walk down the old road.

My footsteps are as silent
as secrets.

I don't look back.

Wassermann meets me
on Charles Bridge,
     as promised.

No one is here
but us.
For the first time,
I miss the clouds of tourists,
their parasols and cameras
held high.

The puddle
around Wassermann's shoes
is bigger
and deeper
than I've ever seen it.
He must have been here a long time,
waiting for me.

(I'm glad
I made him wait.)

Wassermann's expression
rises and falls.
I was afraid
you weren't coming!

I told you I'd be here.
I try for a smile,
hoisting the violin case
in the air.
I should give it back to Wassermann,

but I'm not willing to part
with the beautiful
      (horrible)
thing inside
      just yet.

Wassermann's blind eye
roams across the bridge.
He must be more nervous
than I am.
When a wish comes true,
it never feels
quite
real.
And he must have wished
very hard
for me.

     (Or does
     some part of him know
     he's about to invite
     a girl-wolf
     into his belly?)

Come along,
Wassermann says.
You have a busy lifetime
ahead of you.

I follow the man with no shadow,
the violin case bumping
against my knees,
bruising them purple
as the fading night.

Where I'm going,
I won't ever grow up.
But Wassermann
isn't taking me to Neverland
or Narnia.

We pass the stolen headstones
in Old Town.
They form a black chessboard
and even Wassermann
avoids
walking on them.
He hops over every crack
like a child himself.

We reach the black house
as dawn sweeps over Prague.
It would be so easy to run;
Aunt Žofie wouldn't even know
I'd been gone.

Wassermann frowns
at my wavering steps.
He opens the door,
sweeping a hand
(no claws to be seen)
inside.
Aren't you coming, Ilana?

I'm the girl,
not the monster;
he shouldn't have to
invite me into his home.
But he does.

I fit another smile
onto my lips,
like I'm putting on
a new coat,
one with knives hidden
in its pockets,
and walk
            across
                        the threshold.

I'm a comet tail of a girl,
hurtling toward
the dark center of something
I don't understand.

Stop me
if you've heard this one before:
a musician
descends
into the underworld.

(But the story
doesn't have to end there.)

Chapter Thirty-Five

I wade into the black house
the way I used to wade
into the ocean.
Every step I take
feels too slow.

But Wassermann
moves briskly,
whistling
as he guides me deeper
into his kingdom.
He got what he wanted—
or what he thought he did.

There's a difference, you know.

In the foyer, there are:
four pairs of children's shoes,
and a basket of others,
single sandals and boots
without owners.

How many
other children were here
before Benjamin,
Issur and Lior,
Pearl?
It's a thought
I won't let myself follow
to its end.

The bone structure of Wassermann's house
is too good.
I can see the way one floorboard
fits into the joint of the next.
Like its owner,
the house
must be
starving.

The wallpaper is absinthe green
and I swear
I can see faces in the water stains,
open mouths,

weeping eyes,
hands forever clawing
for solid ground.

The bedroom
Wassermann takes me to
is a nursery.
Toys from every era
are piled in the corners;
half-finished books
lie on the floor.
There are a dozen beds
but only four look slept in,
their sheets rumpled
and warm.

Whispers travel to the ceiling
like smoke from the cigarette
Wassermann lights
with his finger.

Pearl, Lior, and Issur
stare at me
from where they're sitting
on the floor.
They don't know
I've come to free them.

The twins swarm me first.
Ilana! Ilana!
You're here to stay!
Will you play us more music?

They are all smiles,
but for an instant,
their bright eyes
fall on Wassermann
and something within them
folds,
diminishes.

There's only
one person here
who's allowed to take up space.

Pearl is less trusting
than the boys.
Her dying roses flare
a momentary jealous crimson
when Wassermann
skims his fingers
along my collarbone.

I can *feel*
how his breath
knots in his throat.

He must love
how much Pearl
loves *him*
in this moment.

There's no need
to be jealous, Pearl.
Ilana will be
your big sister!
Wassermann smiles.
Won't you like that?

No!
Pearl stuffs her thumb into
her pink mouth.

> (I can't fault her
> for her jealousy.
> If you must live
> with a monster,
> it's safer
> to be adored by him
> above all others.)

I put the violin case
on an empty bed,
and take out the clothing
I've wrapped
Wassermann's instrument in.

I lay a dress on the white sheets,
and see the monster
nod his approval.
A girl who intends to run
doesn't bring
a wardrobe with her.

        (But a girl
               who intends to fight
                    does.)

I feel fingers
brush
against my shoulder.
Their touch
is warm, solid,
real.

I twirl
and see Benjamin
without the haze of death
casting a veil
over the sharpness of his features.
His eyes are so blue;
they're like a shot
to my heart.

In the black house,
more than anywhere,

he and I
are made of endings.
And that's why
I need to kiss him—
so we can have a beginning too.

I close my eyes,
press my lips
against his gently,
like neither of us
weighs more
than a snowflake.

(I was born in 2006.
He was born in 1902.
We've both been
time traveling
so we could meet
in the here and now.)

A whistle cuts us short.
It's tuneless,
but sharp enough to make me
bleed.

Benjamin and I
turn
as one

and Wassermann winks
at us, as if he
and he alone
were privy to our kiss,
as if the others
weren't there
at all.

Now, now,
meine Kinder.
Ilana will have plenty of time
for all of you later.
First, she and I
need to talk.

I don't want
to be alone
with Wassermann
ever
again.
But I have
no choice.

Chapter Thirty-Six

Wassermann's office
is so mundane
that it makes me dizzy.

The room is all cherrywood
and softly glowing lamps.
Walls of books
on poetry,
astronomy,
history
press in on us,
making the space feel
like a set of lungs
contracting.

Wassermann throws himself
into the armchair
behind his shipwreck of a desk.
There's so much jetsam
splashed across it,
I don't know where to begin
looking for the teapot
he keeps
the souls of the dead inside.

But it must be here
somewhere.

Wassermann opens a book at random,
the pages rippling
like waves.
As the only living child here,
you'll have special responsibilities,
he declares,
like a father—
or a general.
But I imagine
you'll love
being an older sister.
Being an only child
is so lonely.
I should know—
I was one
myself.

My smile
is vanilla sweet.
I won't have to be lonely now.
It's like in Peter Pan.
I'm Wendy Darling.

Shadows collect
in the fine lines

around Wassermann's mouth,
but none dare
touch him.
They, too,
must be wary of his appetite.
I'm afraid I haven't
read that book.

I'm made up of even older tales
than Wassermann can imagine.
My People
left Egypt,
traveled to the land
of milk and honey,
were banished
to the wilds
of Babylon,
Germany,
Poland
a thousand years
before the Grimms
set their stories
down on paper.

My People's tale
is old as time.
And it is *strong*.

Wassermann spreads
his January-white hands
on either side of my face, smiling.

Soon, I will take your death
and hide it
inside a needle,
an egg,
a duck,
a rabbit,
guarded by a wolf
on an island
far from here.

You will never sleep
inside a glass coffin;
your bones will never crumble
like sugar cubes.
You
and I
will live
until this world ends
and another
opens its pages.

I am sixteen,
but I want
to be eighteen,

thirty-six,
ninety-six,
and counting.
I want to see everything
this world
             (and the next)
have to offer.

But what falls from my lips
is another lie.
Good.
I never want to get old.

Wassermann rubs at his
(dead)
(white)
eye.
His fingers
come away,
damp with liquid
thicker
than tears.
Is there blood in his veins
or does he carry a river
with him, always?
You don't have to worry, Ilana.
You'll never have to grow up now.

(It's a promise
I know
Wassermann will keep
if I'm not careful.)

In a house full of children,
there are always
bangs,
clatters,
shrieks of delight
and dismay.
Just because
the kids here are dead
doesn't make them
an exception.

So when one of the twins
screams,
Wassermann sighs.
He does such a good impression
of the put-upon uncle
that a corner of my heart
almost falls
for the act.
*I'll be back
in a moment,* he says.

The darkness itself
writhes around Wassermann
as he passes me.

I race
to the other side of the desk,
opening each drawer
as slowly
as my shaking fingers
will let me.

I need to find the teapot.
But what excuse
could I give Wassermann
if he catches me now?
I've run out of lies;
I've used them all up
getting this far.

What I discover
in the monster's desk:
coins from dead empires;
a bestiary,
many-legged monsters marked
as *sister*,
as *brother*.
But there's no teapot
to be seen.

Outside, I hear
the man with no shadow
lecturing Lior and Issur,
his voice droning
on
and on.

I'm about to return
to my seat
when my eyes settle
on the book
Wassermann's been poring over.

This must be
how Pandora felt
when she was confronted
with the box of her undoing.

I reach for it anyway.

On the first page
is a sketch:
a hollow-eyed girl.
I don't recognize her,
but I know the hand
that drew her.
It is unmistakably Benjamin's.

The second drawing
is of a boy,
his face gaunt,
a famine victim
in his final days.
As I meet the boy's longing gaze,
I start to understand.

Each page in the book
contains another drawing
of another
dead
child,
eaten
one memory
at a time
by Rudolf Wassermann.

The pages go on
and on.
Five children,
ten,
twelve—
soon, I lose count
the way I did
when I tried to read
the names of the dead
on the walls of Pinkas Synagogue.

The numbers
overwhelm me.
And so do
the eyes.

I'm staring
at the death rattle of a soul,
catalogued,
a collection of souvenirs
grimmer than any bag of bones.

These drawings are Benjamin's
memorial to the children
                    swallowed
by Wassermann.
But I believe
our monster
keeps the sketches
for a far different reason:
he is gloating
over his stolen eternity.

Anger that goes past red
and into the black
floods my head,
a dam broken
into a thousand
                jagged
                        pieces.

Each pair of shoes
in the foyer
was worn by a child
Wassermann took from the cemetery.
I know their faces now,
but they are lost
to me
and every world.

Chapter Thirty-Seven

The squeak of wet shoes
warns me of Wassermann's approach.
I turn the book
back to its awful beginning.

If I kill Wassermann,
isn't that the same
as destroying
whatever holds
the souls of Benjamin and the others?

Won't his death
also set the children free?

Benjamin knows my heart
has a new crack in it
the instant
I stumble
out of Wassermann's office.

Is there a place
we can be alone?
I try to sound
like a girl
who wants a kiss
and nothing more.

Benjamin excels
at the game of survival.
The roses braided around his wrist
turn red with love and need.
But his eyes
remain unclouded.

He guides me
down the corridor,
tracing his finger
along the walls as we go.
A door that was not there before
creaks open beside us,
a (temporary)
sanctuary.

The space
we slip into is small;
it presses our ribs together.
I am Eve;
he is Adam.
We spring from each other
and the feeling of Benjamin's cheek
against mine
is like coming home.

The shoes with no owners, I manage.
All those kids.
I didn't understand
before now.
I didn't understand
how many ghosts
Wassermann has eaten.

I double over,
grabbing
a fistful of Benjamin's shirt.
I pour
my screams into cloth
a century old.

My hands
feel weaker than they ever did
in the cemetery.

Why did I think
I could do this?

Tell me about
the lost world, I beg.
Tell me a memory
Wassermann hasn't torn out of you.
Give me an anchor
so he can't pull me
out to sea.

My little sister's name was Helena.
And I'm glad she sailed
across the ocean
before the war began, Benjamin says.
Helena might have become
an actress,
a fashion designer,
a doctor,
as my father
intended me to be.
Helena isn't
sixteen forever.
Helena got to choose.

Forever
isn't supposed to be
an ugly word.

But here,
it is.

There are no prayers to carry us back
into this tomb of a house,
no Psalms
that can scrub my face
free of salt
and rage.

But Benjamin and I
have to go back.
We need to keep pretending.

The music coming from the office
buries itself
like a needle
       (like a fever)
in me
as we enter Wassermann's domain
       (again)
but this time,
Benjamin and I
go together.

      (We've always been stronger
              when we're together.)

Wassermann and I sit
side by side
as Benjamin draws us.

The monster
smooths his hair,
tilts his head to the side,
raises his chin high
so that the curve of his jaw
is blade sharp.
He's practiced this pose
in front of his reflection—
I can tell.

No living creature
         (other than me)
will ever see this portrait,
but Benjamin
still makes it flattering,
smoothing away
Wassermann's faults
until he looks
like a hero
who recently stepped from
the stanzas of a poem.

In this moment,
Benjamin is nothing more
than Wassermann's magic mirror.

My gaze skitters
to a letter opener
on the desk.

The blade is as dull
as unrequited love.
But my hand begins
edging
toward it nonetheless.

I've never hurt anyone.
I've never done battle
in an alleyway
or on a playground.
But I can almost feel
the weight of the blade
in my palm.

The little knife
would fit so perfectly
in Wassermann's
swan-white neck.

My fingers
close
around
the hilt of the letter opener
when—

Snap.
Benjamin's pencil lies
broken on the page.
Black swirls of graphite
leave scars
along the softness of his palm.

His eyes say
what he can't
as Wassermann pins him
      (a butterfly to a corkboard)
with a glare
that paralyzes us both.

In Benjamin's silence, I hear:
You're not fast enough
to kill him.
Not
like
this.

He's right—
I'd fail,
an Orpheus in every way,
careless in my haste,
my desperation to feel the sun
on my face again.

But what I wouldn't do
to strip Rudolf Wassermann
of everything.

My life
lies in two parts now:
before
      Benjamin, Wassermann,
      the cemetery
      that revealed them both
and after
      the kisses,
      the violin,
      the truth.

I waver in the haze of *after*
while Benjamin
finishes drawing
his portrait.

There are faces in the walls.
I try
not to look.
I try
not to see
how much they resemble
the dead kids
in Wassermann's book.

Chapter Thirty-Eight

Dad once told me
there are two theories
about the size of the universe.

Some scientists say
it's getting smaller—
a bubble about to pop.
The other theory says
it's expanding—
a library
that won't stop adding stories
to its shelves.

My universe
is shrinking
inside the black house;
there are only
so many rooms
I can wander through
      (always looking for souls)
and Wassermann's views
are as narrow
as his hallways.

One idea
could bring
the entire thing
down.

There is a window
at the end of the hall
looking out
across a darkened square.

If I peer through it,
I could almost
be back in Prague.
I glimpse spires
cutting through the mist
and hear the toll of far-off bells.

But there's no one outside
and the sky
is empty.
There's no second star
I can use
as true north.
And when I try to open the window,
the latch sticks.

What are you doing?
Wassermann's voice
forces me to step back.

I turn,
assembling
another smile for his benefit.
I just wanted
a taste of the night air.

You can't be
homesick already!
Wassermann
folds his hands
over mine, as if to keep me
from flying away
like a true Wendy-bird.
What is out in the world
that you can't find here?
We
are
all
you
need.

I don't shiver.

If Wassermann
is a river,
I'm a stone;
I won't be moved
by his power.

Supper at Aunt Žofie's
meant cucumbers so green
they looked like
the first day of spring,
fever-red tomatoes,
kulajda soup with sprigs of dill,
and fat pierogi
stuffed with potatoes.
She was careful
not to mix meat
and dairy
or give me pig.

But I don't think
I can expect that
from Wassermann.

The twins lead me
down the hall to the dining room
later that night—
or day.

       (Who can tell?
       There's no sunlight here,
       no way for me to know
       how much time has passed
       in Wassermann's kingdom.)

The boys hold hands,
as if they're afraid
of tumbling
over the edge of the known world
without each other.

I can't help but say:
I didn't think
you needed to eat.

I'm too close
to their deaths again,
but the twins
don't seem to care.
They shrug as one.
I don't think Lior
and Issur
plan to do everything
in unison.
But they've been
beside each other for so long
that their hearts
and thoughts
are braided together
like their fingers.

I like dinner, says Issur.
It's almost
like being alive again.

Who were you,
>   I ask,
when you were *alive?*

The rabbi's grandsons.
Lior's voice
warms with pride.
We were going to be rabbis too—
studying Torah,
Talmud,
learning to speak with angels.

What was
your grandfather's name?

At this question,
Issur and Lior exchange
a look,
pale brows crinkling
like sheets of paper.
Then Issur says:
You know,
>   *we don't remember*
>   *anymore.*

Pomegranates and apples,
seeded things
intent on trapping me

in this labyrinth,
are laid out on a long dusty table.
Each piece of fruit
looks made of still water
from Wassermann's river.

He clears his throat,
his straight-backed posture
conveying
a series of commands:
no elbows on the table,
knees together,
ankles crossed,
now let us pray.

The dead kids say:
Baruch ata Adonai,
Eloheinu Melech ha-olam,
bo're p'ri ha'etz.

In this garden of unearthly delights,
I can't trust anything.
But I have to wipe
the drool
off my chin.

What

      has Wassermann
           done
               to
      me?

I know you must be confused.
Wassermann rolls an apple
the color of tears
across his open palm.
When real food
has rotted away,
this *is what's left.*
A memory of desire,
slightly fainter
than the real thing—
much like a ghost itself.

He winks at me,
like this is a wonder,
not a horror.
He's long past the point
where he can
tell the difference.

I'm alive, I try.
I'm human.
I can't live on the shadows

of what used to be
like the dead can.

Wassermann's breath
is dragon-fire hot
against my cheek.
Oh, but you can.
There's a trick to it—
an art form.
I promised
I'd teach you everything.
Be patient!
I will.

The twins each take an apple
and sink their teeth
into its crystal skin.
The inside of the fruit
is phantom white.
Does it have *any* taste?
Can a memory
hold on to that much?

I watch the dead eat,
my own belly
twisting in hunger.

Wassermann's eyes
are half-lidded,

but I don't think
for a second
that he isn't drinking up
my expression
with his wine.

Is he looking
for an excuse to transform me
into just another sketch in the book
bound in Benjamin's tears?

I keep my face
as tranquil
as Ophelia's must have been
when she lay back
and let the water
take her.

Chapter Thirty-Nine

It's Pearl
who Wassermann lures
away from the table
and into the office.
He takes her hand;
she beams at him,

the favorite once more.
But it is I
who am his
(un)willing
accomplice.

When the door is locked,
Wassermann forces me
into a chair.
His hands
feel sharp as swords
when they come down
on my shoulders.
I'll teach you
a new trick now.
It's really not so difficult.

Protest surges
up my throat,
but it's too late for me
to pull away.
Wassermann pries my mouth open
using two fingers.

Then
it
begins.

The taste of Pearl
reminds me
of burnt caramel.
It sticks
to the roof of my mouth,
sealing my lips
shut,
keeping my screams
locked up tight.

I gag
on life,
on potential,
on years
the little girl
never got to live.

I want to vomit,
but the only thing
filling my stomach is a memory.

Home means
      (*meant*)
so many things to Pearl.
An apartment
with peeling tea-colored wallpaper,
a cloud-soft rabbit toy
tucked into bed beside her,
the taste of hot cocoa on a winter's day.

But most of all, it meant
the June warmth of being held
by a woman
who smelled of fresh, sweet bread.

The woman
          (her mother)
twirls
Pearl around their living room,
an aria of laughter
accompanying their dance.
They are two ballerinas in a music box,
trapped in a moment
that ended long ago.

But *in* this moment,
Pearl knows
          she is safe,
          she is loved.
And she believes these things
          will be true
          for all time.

I lift my head—
and wish
I hadn't.
Pearl's edges are worn,
ripped,

shredded
in all
the wrong places.

She's a pastel girl now,
smudged,
incomplete,
less real
than even ordinary ghosts.
I can see her ribs
peeking out
from under her skin.

Pearl doesn't have long
left in this world.
or any other.

You can go.
Wassermann dismisses Pearl
with a wave of his hand,
a conductor
who has tired
of his instrument.

The little girl
drifts from the room,
silent,
exhausted,

more confused
than ever.

Benjamin was right.
She doesn't understand
what Wassermann takes from her.

She won't understand
until it's too late.

Wassermann pulls me to my feet
effortlessly.
I feel light in his arms,
my bones as hollow
as a raven's.

The man with no shadow
strokes my hair,
gentle as the lovers
he'll make sure
I never have.
Not to worry, Ilana.
It's a bit much at first.
But you'll get used to it.
You'll have forever
to adjust, after all.

I want
to howl,
to wail.
But no sound
rises in my throat.

Go and get the violin,
will you? Wassermann says.
I'd like to hear some music
now that we've eaten.

My People
have always been forced to entertain
our demons,
buying another hour,
another day,
another precious
few
breaths.

So I play
rage
and ruination.

I play
to bring the walls
of the black house
down.

Chapter Forty

Benjamin finds me
after my twisted concert.
I can't look at him.
Not after what Wassermann
made me do.
Not when I can still
taste Pearl
in my mouth.

(I couldn't look at *her*, either,
when I returned the black violin
to its case in the nursery.)

Benjamin takes me back
to the closet he made,
holding me
even as I struggle
against him.

I say:
I'm going to kill Wassermann.
I'm going to get the teapot
and break him with it.
I'm so sorry, Benjamin.

I'm so sorry
this has been happening
to all of you
for so long.

He threads his fingers
through my hair.
I'll distract Wassermann.
I'll take him to another part
of the house.
I'll say I need better lighting
to draw him by.
Then you can find
where he's keeping
our souls.
Then—

Our plan collapses
the way I wish
this house would.
It ends
with a short cry
and Pearl's fawn-light footsteps
as she runs
from our hiding spot.

When we're about to die,
we're supposed to say
the Shema.

(Sh'ma Yisra'eil,
Adonai Eloheinu,
Adonai echad.)
As the door of Wassermann's office
bangs
open
and he approaches,
I wonder if
I should say it now.

I've never felt more
like my ancestors,
hiding in a closet
with so much fire
burning in my heart
I'm afraid
the light
will give me away.

The closet door opens
to Wassermann and Pearl
framed
by lamplight.

Pearl tugs
on the sleeve of Wassermann's jacket.
The fabric goes
up and down,

like the cord
of a bell
that rings out
only one message:
> Found you,
> found you,
> found you.

I told you, says Pearl.
I told you
they were being bad,
Onkel Wassermann.
I told you
they were planning
to take me
away from you.

Wassermann
rolls his sleeves up
with two elegant flicks of his wrist.
When he speaks,
his voice
is terribly quiet.
Pearl, will you wait
in the nursery
with the twins?

Benjamin slides in front of me,
his chin already arched
to take the blow
he believes
(or *knows*)
is coming.

Stop!
My voice
is the loudest thing
the room has heard
since Benjamin and I
drew up our plan in whispers.
I push Benjamin aside,
rougher than I want to be.

It was *my idea.*
Benjamin is too good
to think of betraying you
on his own.
You should know that, Wassermann.
I'm more like you
than he's ever been.

I show my girl-wolf teeth
in anger, not fear,
and Wassermann
stops

like a watch
that has run
out of time.

Benjamin stands up
beside me,
ready to deny
what I've said.
But we all know
my words
hold too much truth.

Wassermann snarls
and grabs me
by the end of my braid,
hauling me
out of the closet,
away from the boy
who can't save me.

My hair parts
from my scalp
and I feel
more like Samson
than Delilah,
my courage crumbling.

Wassermann drags me
down the hall,
my feet kicking uselessly
against the floorboards.

I hear Benjamin
cry out
behind us.
But it's too late.
It always was.

I'm drowning
in the legends of my father's city
and I don't know how to swim
back to the surface.

Chapter Forty-One

I should be angry at Pearl,
but I can't help
feeling sorry for her.

It's not her fault
the world
broke her
and that Wassermann

was the one
who glued all her pieces
back together.

The little ghost
must have left the office door open
when she came to sell us out;
Wassermann pushes me
easily inside.
He locks the door
against Benjamin
      and anyone else
      who might try to rescue me
before flinging me
into the nearest chair.

My hip
smashes
against the armrest,
but that's not important.

Because when I glance
at Wassermann's desk,
I finally see the teapot
I've been searching for,
resting on a tower of books.
I don't think anything
can be that full of light
without holding souls.

I have to be calm.
If I am quick,
if I am clever,
I can get the teapot
and change
everything.

Wassermann circles me,
his eyes
growing darker,
his teeth
lengthening
by the second.

I picture his heart
covered in blisters
and black mold.
I'll never reach a heart like that,
no matter what I say.

I
let
you
into
my
HOUSE!
And this
is how

you repay
ME!

Each of Wassermann's
words
fall
like the blows
his fists
must be itching
to deliver.

I point at the door,
toward the nursery.
You can't keep those kids here!
You can't break off
little pieces of their souls
and stuff them into your mouth
like cookies.
Why can't you
let them go?

I give them
a home
and they pay me
in kind!
Wassermann's screams
make the walls shake.
They're nothing anyway—

there are hundreds, thousands
of children just like them!
I'm one of the few real fairy tales
left in the world.
I deserve to keep living.
I matter
and
they
don't!

Wassermann's hateful words
are too much for me.
       I have

             to act

                now.

I lunge like an arrow
loosed from a bow,
like a wolf set free
in the forest,
and grab the teapot
off Wassermann's desk.

The air whistles
as he tries to seize my hair
a second time.
But Benjamin was wrong—
I am quicker
than Wassermann is.

I shout:
You're never
going to hurt
anyone
again!

The teapot
feels better than a knife
in the burning spread of my hand
as I hurl it
against the wall
with all my might.

> Let there be light,
> let there be life,
> let there be an end
> to all this.

The shards of the teapot fall,
but nothing inside of them
stirs.

As they rain down,
Wassermann bursts out
laughing,
holding his sides
like he's about to come undone.
Ilana, Ilana, Ilana,

he chants, like a spell.
Did you really think
I would be stupid enough
to keep the souls of my children
in plain sight?
Did you really think
you could free them as easily as that?
Do you think others
haven't tried?

Shock leeches
my swiftness,
my hope,
as a new realization
pins me down.

I'm Persephone,
trapped in the darkness
with no means
to claw my way back
to anyone
I love.

Wassermann tips my chin up
and kisses me.

The kiss is brutal,
hurricane furious;

there's no love
in the act—
or in Wassermann himself.
But the monster takes more
than my mouth
in his.

I feel myself
falling
away
the closer
he gets.

I remember:
the first time I held a violin.
I was six years old,
and the notes
came as easily as breath.

I feel the memory,
the piece of me,
vanish, torn free,
a scratched-out poem
from my book of life.
I feel the hole
it leaves behind,
empty, bloody, sore—
as if I've lost a tooth.

If you won't work with me,
then you will work for me, hisses Wassermann.
Your life is as good
as any other's.
And it certainly
will nourish me.

I can see it clearly now:
if Wassermann can't have me,
he'll destroy me.
That's what weak people *do.*

And the most impressive monsters
are always the least impressive men.

Chapter Forty-Two

Once, the city of Prague
rose up against the Nazis,
a chorus of resistance.

When Benjamin
crashes into the office,
a tempest of a boy,
his arrival is as loud
as that artillery fire.

The bones
in my wrist
grind against his
as he pulls me back
from Wassermann.
Together,
we topple
into the corridor.

The faces
in the wood
blur together.
There is anger
in the echoes of suffering
that reverberate
through this house.

Benjamin yells:
This is our home too,
Wassermann!

The office door swings shut.
Its edges break down,
as if they were made of sand,
leaving nothing
but smooth wood paneling
in its place.

We're not safe;
we're not free.
The lock Benjamin made
won't hold for long.
The walls are already
rattling in time
with Wassermann's screams.

Benjamin—
this might be the last time
I ever get to say his name.
I want to savor it,
but there's no time *left*.

He grips my arms
and I see a flash of the man
he could have been.
He would have fought
with fists or poetry
against the dark tide
that swept over Prague
decades after
he was laid to rest.

(He shouldn't have died
so young.
Prague needed Benjamin
and so did our People.)

You need to go,
Benjamin says.
You need to run.

What about you?

Benjamin shakes his head
slowly,
as if it's heavy
with all the lives
he could have lived.
It's too late for me,
for any of us.
But it's not too late
for you.
Please, Ilana.
Go home.
Live.
Do it for me.

The office door begins taking shape again.
A knob grows from the wall,
a black flower
I can't uproot.

Then the door
comes
crashing
open.

Wassermann's humanity
has slipped away
entirely.
He lurches
into the hallway,
hair plastered
to his brow with sweat.
His eyes are voids
even the centuries
can't fill.

He throws himself
at me with a shriek,
but Benjamin catches his tormentor
before Wassermann's hands
can wrap themselves
around my throat.

The boy and the monster
slam
onto the ground.
The black house
barely shivers.
Violence is all
it has ever known.

Benjamin seizes Wassermann
by the collar of his fine suit,

and his fist
> connects
>> with
the *vodník*'s face.

The fury that moves
over Benjamin's features
is not born of hate;
it's born of love.
For me.
For Issur and Lior.
For Pearl.
For every child
he couldn't save.

Wassermann smiles,
> ravenous,
through the blood in his mouth.
You can't win!
You'll never win!
This is my house, boy,
and you
are only
another thing
I own.

Benjamin
raises his head.

He knows the monster
is telling the truth;
he can't defeat Wassermann.
But still he says:
Ilana,
RUN!

I didn't want
to say goodbye
like *this*.

But if I stay,
Wassermann
will destroy us
with our love for each other.

So
I run.

Interlude V:
Wassermann

When I'm done with Benjamin,
there won't be enough of him left
to scatter
across the Vltava.

I am going
to feel
that brat
break
beneath my hands
if it's the last thing
I ever
do.

And I'm going
to make Ilana
watch.

Chapter Forty-Three

I'm spinning
down the hallway,
music I can't understand
crackling like fire
in my head,
notes I'll hear
until the day I die.
I tried—
and I failed,
completely.

Orpheus *always* fails.

But it's the thought
of the man
with his lyre
        (who sang his way
        into Hell
        more sweetly
        than I did)
that finally
        makes me
                stop.

His instrument
was his weapon,
the place where he stored
his agony,
his love,
his very soul.

And
at
once
I know
where Wassermann
has hidden
the souls of the dead,
why each time
I played
the black violin,
I grew stronger
and hungrier
than before.

Magic will burn
you
up.

But I won't burn
for Wassermann
anymore.

I race back to the nursery.
But the black violin,
the source of everything
Wassermann is,
isn't where I left it
sleeping in its case
on one of the beds.

It's in Pearl's arms.

The twins
have taken shelter
beneath a bed.
They cover their ears
and shut their eyes tightly,
wishing themselves
anywhere
but here.

I want to comfort the boys,
but I need to use
the few words I have
to set them *free*.

Pearl, I say.

The strawberry girl
hugs the violin against her chest,

like another child
would cradle a doll.
You can't have it!
If you take it,
you'll take me away
from Onkel Wassermann!

Wassermann doesn't love you.
I hate bringing this truth to her;
it's a basket of vipers
I lay at her feet.
But I have to.
He's keeping you
from your family,
from people
who wouldn't ever
steal parts of you
to keep themselves
alive.

Pearl snaps:
Onkel Wassermann
is my only family.

I open the story of Pearl's old life.
             (I can't
               give it back to her,
               but I can do this much.)

Once upon a time,
you had a toy rabbit,
an apartment in Old Town,
a history to call your own.
You had a mother
    who danced with you,
    who laughed with you,
    who never frightened you.
She was your home
and you were hers.

Wassermann stole
your mother *from you*
and you from her.

Pearl stares at me,
a veil of impossible tears
glittering in her eyes.
Does she feel the emptiness
where the memories of her mother
and her life
should be?
I think
she must.

I kneel in front of her.
Pearl,
there were other kids here.

You knew *them.*
Maybe they were even
your friends.
And now
they're gone.
But you don't have to vanish.
Too many have already.
Please, Pearl. Please.

I hold my hand out
and close my eyes.
I won't take the violin
from her.

Too much
has been taken
from her
already.

Lior and I
don't remember home either.
Issur's voice
creeps out from under the bed,
even if he
is too frightened to.
But I remember
playing
with Miriam, Jan, and Moshe,

eating dinner
with Hana and Eva and Oskar.
And I remember
when they all disappeared
from the nursery.

It's scary here sometimes, Lior says,
his eyes as wide
as open doors.
And I don't think
home
is supposed to be scary.

Pearl whispers:
I want to know
why I feel lost.
I want to know
why I feel smaller and smaller.
I want to go home …
but I'm not sure where
home is *anymore.*
It's with these words
that Pearl surrenders.

She puts the black violin
in my arms
and I feel its power
rising to meet
my fingertips.

I don't have time
to hug Pearl.
But I do anyway,
crushing her
against my chest,
this butterfly-fragile child
whose girlhood was devoured
by too many monsters.

When you are a final girl,
        you run
            for all the girls
                who never made it this far.

Chapter Forty-Four

I reach the foyer of the black house
with its graveyard of shoes
as Wassermann and Benjamin
appear
at the top of the stairs.

The monster descends,
his fury so hot
I'm surprised it doesn't
burn us to ash.

Wassermann's hand is curled
like a tree root
over Benjamin's shoulder.
The boy's arm is twisted
at an ugly angle;
the blue of his eyes is bruised
with despair.
He believes
I wasn't fast enough,
that he couldn't rescue me.

I wish
I could kiss hope
back into his mouth.
I wish
I could tell him
everything.

But there's no time.

Do you have any idea who I am?
Do you have any idea
what I'm going to do to you?
Wassermann screams.

And
I
laugh.

The Ghosts of Rose Hill

I can't help it.

I don't care
who you are.
I don't care
what you're calling yourself.
You're Bluebeard.
You're Sauron.
You're Hannibal Lecter.
You're el Viejo del Saco.
You're the valley of Gehenna,
always hungry
for something new
to stuff
into your black mouth.

And the only part
of the story
you matter in
is the part
where someone
like me
beats
someone
like you.

Ilana, come here!
You'll only make this worse
if you don't!
Wassermann bellows.

The walls of the black house
shudder.
But I don't move.
There's nothing left
to pull me toward him,
no reason for me
to obey.

Ilana!
Wassermann stamps his foot
like he's Pearl's age.
Come here!
Now!

I grip the neck
of the black violin
so hard
that the strings
bite into my fingers.
But I smile.

Wassermann's anger crumbles
like dried rose petals.

There's some new emotion
writing itself
across his face.
He finally understands
he's been wrong
all along.
He has
no power
over me.

My soul
is still
my own,
and my love
is not weakness—
it's my strength.

I swing the violin
like a sword
intent on burying itself
deep inside
the belly of a beast.

It strikes the wall;
the impact travels
up
my
spine

into
the deepest part
of
me.

The broken violin
erupts
in light
and the black house
exhales,
a living thing
filled with relief
as its timbers snap,
its wallpaper tears,
its ceilings sag
beneath the weight
of time.

I see dawn
outside the nearest window
as the glass
cracks down the center.
But it isn't until
the light bulbs above me
shatter
that I run,
Benjamin at my side.

Pearl and the twins
rush down
the lurching stairs.
Even their fear
      (or love)
of Wassermann
is not enough to keep them here.

Benjamin and I
pull the children close.
It's going to be all right,
he assures them,
an older brother
to the end.

The front door sticks
when I try to open it,
the wood
suddenly warped
with all the ages
it has seen.
Panic dances
in my chest
before I dig
my heels in
and wrench it open.

The dead and I spill
back into the real world,
where the monsters
know to sheath their claws.

The symphony
of destruction
ends
abruptly.
The black house
gives way,
the crunch
of rotten wood
like bone
as it
comes
tumbling
down.

I'm no knight,
but I think
I may have just
slain a dragon.

Chapter Forty-Five

I turn to see
Benjamin,
Pearl, Issur, Lior
illuminated.
Not by the sun
pouring through the clouds,
but by something greater.
Our eyes meet
over the blaze
of this newly kindled light.

One by one,
the ghosts flicker and fade,
their smiles
shining with hope
they didn't dare have before.

Benjamin cups my face
in his hands.
Galaxies pour
from the tips of his fingers,
bleeding stars so blue
they could be
the deepest part of a flame.

In this moment,
we're closer
than we've ever been
and farther apart.

I've known what was coming
ever since the blue-eyed boy and I
watched the stars
wheeling overhead
in my aunt's garden.
But who can prepare themselves
for an ending?

I want to tell Benjamin:
Wait.
I want to beg him:
Stay with me for all time.
What I whisper instead:
I love you, Benjamin.

The outlines of his hands
have begun to blur.
But Benjamin's grin is as wide
as the world
he is about to leave behind.

Ilana—
ikh hab dir lib.
Ilana—
miluji tě.
Ilana—
Ich liebe dich.
Ilana—
I love you.

Then he
      and the other children
              vanish
into the light.

Chapter Forty-Six

The black house is dead;
the souls who were caged
in it are free.
But Wassermann
is very much alive,
coughing
and shaking the dust
of his ruined home
from his dark hair.

He holds his trembling hands
in front of widening eyes.
The veins
collecting at his wrists
aren't silver anymore.
They're blue—
like mine.

Without the souls,
without the children,
without anyone
but himself,
Rudolf Wassermann
is perfectly ordinary—
and perfectly human.

What did you do?
he screams.
What did you do to me?

Wassermann may be
taller than I am,
but I feel like
I'm looking down
at *him*.
You're mortal now,
I tell him.
You'll live

and you'll die
like anyone else.
Maybe it's time
you started acting
like a human being.

Wassermann pulls his arm back,
ready to strike me,
when a man's voice calls out:
You!
What are you doing
with that girl?

The
(ex) monster and I
both turn.
A man stands in the bakery doorway
a few buildings away,
his arms weighed down
with fresh bread.

I've never
seen him before,
but when he charges
toward Wassermann,
I know
I'll remember
his face

     (his map of wrinkles,
     his drooping mustache,
     even the smudge of flour
     on his nose)
for the rest of my life.

The baker asks me:
Is this man
bothering you?
Do I need to call the police?

There's no trouble!
None at all!
Wassermann is breathless
as he straightens his jacket.
     (Or tries to.
     There are two hundred years
     of wrinkles
     caught in the cloth.)
He retreats,
a dusty young man
in a city
where thousands of others
just like him
are about to begin
their days.

Wassermann would have hurt me
if he'd had the chance.
He might try again
when there's no good neighbor
to chase him away.
But I'm too tired to worry
about tomorrow;
I only want to thank my rescuer
and return home.

Chapter Forty-Seven

Every step
on my walk back to Aunt Žofie's
takes a year;
every mile
takes a lifetime.

I duck beneath
the Old Town Bridge Tower,
where Benjamin and I
first kissed,
reaching for where
he should be
beside me
and finding nothing
but the cool morning air.

Benjamin's gone.
The World to Come
is his home now.

And as this truth
sinks into my heart,
that's when
the tears
finally
come.

I don't stop crying
until I reach
the Rose Hill cemetery,
and that's only because
I can't anymore.

There's blood
in my veins,
not water.
I'm no mermaid,
no *rusalka*,
no *vodník*.
I have to follow
my own advice to Wassermann:
I have to be a human girl
and not
someone else's myth.

Without Benjamin,
Rose Hill cemetery feels empty—
a body
without a soul,
a harp
without its strings.

But the bluebirds still sing;
the wind still whispers its Psalms
over the *matzevot*.
They don't know
about Benjamin,
Pearl,
Lior and Issur,
or any of the others
buried here.

I set a stone
on top of Benjamin's grave,
and guide my fingers
over the broken branch
etched above his name.

The sound of a real branch
snapping
pulls me to my feet.
I fumble for the stone
belonging to Benjamin's memory.

(I don't think
he'd mind
if I used it in self-defense.)

But Wassermann
        (or some
        lesser monster)
hasn't come for me.

The newcomer is only an old man,
as alive as the flowers
in my aunt's garden.
I breathe out
a sigh.
I'm safe.

I've come to this hillside
many times,
stumbling around the trees,
searching for the graves
of my family, says the man.
The fringes of his tallit
sway in the breeze.
But I only found them today.
Do you know who cleared
this cemetery?

My voice shakes
when I tell him:
I did.

I've never seen
another living person here;
I was always alone
with Prague's dead
and my own.
But it feels good to share this place
with someone who understands
how important it is.

There's a gloss of tears
in the man's eyes
as he stands beside me.
He doesn't take
my hands in his
or stroke
my ragged knuckles.
That's fine.
I'm not ready to be touched,
not after Wassermann.

Thank you, the old man says.
Thank you for giving this place
back its life.

We gaze at Benjamin's headstone
and the man's lips move
as he forms the letters.
Do you know
who he was?
This Benjamin?

Here is what
spills out of me:
Benjamin died
too young.
He was kind.
He drew the things
he saw in his dreams.
He couldn't dance
but he could sing,
and he was as brave
as Prague's white lion.

He sounds extraordinary,
the old man says.
It's too bad
you and I
will not meet him
in this world.

Yeah, I whisper.
It is.

Chapter Forty-Eight

In the kitchen of Rose Cottage,
I feed Aunt Žofie
the story of what happened
during the dawn
that seemed to last for days.

She slumps back
in her seat,
as if the meal is too dark
and rich
to stomach.
And the vodník?
Where is he?

Out there,
somewhere.
Human …
and broken.
I wanted to destroy him,
but I think living
might be a better punishment.

Aunt Žofie hides
the knife of her smile

behind the teacup
she lifts to her lips.
She may not be a Lopez,
but there is still plenty of wolf in her.
Sometimes
the cruelest thing of all
is mercy.
He'll live
       and grow old
            and die.
But what
are you
going to do now, Ilana?

The honest answer
is also the shortest one.
Live, I guess.
Make music
even if my parents disapprove.
Life is too short,
too precious
to waste it
fitting yourself
into someone else's design.
And I'll remember
the dead and the lost,
even if no one else does.

Aunt Žofie's kiss
is butterfly soft
against my temple.
Good answers.

I can't explain to my friends
(exactly)
what happened this summer;
I can't talk to them
about the time I spent
inside the black house.
But I should tell them
               something
after so many weeks
             of silence.

I'm sorry
I disappeared.
I was dealing
with a lot.
I didn't mean to ignore you.

I don't hover
around my phone,
waiting
for Sarah's
or Martina's
responses.

But I promise myself,
when they do reply,
I'll try
telling more of the truth
than not.

What I email my parents:
A declaration:

> *I believe*
> *in myself;*
> *I believe*
> *in the extraordinary places*
> *my music will take me.*
> *Please,*
> *believe in me too.*

What I attach to the letter:
a video of me
playing the black violin.

> *Trust that I've learned*
> *how to protect myself*
> *from what you're afraid*
> *may be lying in wait for me*
> *in the future.*
> *Trust me*
> *and my choices.*

The response I receive:
>*We're talking to your aunt.*
>*She told us*
>*about what you've done*
>*in the cemetery.*
>*She's impressed*
>*by how responsible you've been*
>*this summer.*

>*Maybe*
>*we can compromise*
>*about your music*
>*when you come home.*

Chapter Forty-Nine

If this were a movie
>(and it isn't,
>even if what happened
>in the black house
>feels like a dream now)
I'd walk away in triumph
and never have to talk
to Rudolf Wassermann again.

But Prague feels small,
so it doesn't surprise me
when I see Wassermann
on the shore of the Vltava
when September rises
and I'm on the verge
of returning home.

The monster
　　　(no more)
waves his hands about
as he tries to tell a pair of tourists
how to use the swan boat
they've rented.

His nose is red,
raw,
peeling,
his shirt faded
from being washed
too many times.
He doesn't look
like an emperor
or a legend
anymore.
He looks
like a painting
that has spent too much time
in the sun.

I should feel vindicated.
Wassermann has been brought low.
But when he catches
my eye,
I see hate
burning so brightly
it could outshine
every candle in St. Vitus Cathedral
and Staronová synagoga.

I go to him anyway.

You.
He spits the word,
sounding hoarse,
sick,
tired,
human.

I answer:
Me.

But Wassermann's old ways
are slow to die
and it's a curse he hisses,
over my head
and the cradles of the children
I've barely begun to dream of.

You live beside the sea—
I know that much, Ilana.
And there are only
so many cities beside oceans,
where the people look like you,
speak like you.
One day, when you're not expecting me,
I'll come for you
and whatever children
you may have.

I don't allow myself to blink.
I imagine
I'm Bruncvík's white lion,
unmoved,
unafraid
in the face of something hateful
and wretched.

I've been in a story
long enough to understand
this much:
a curse
can be broken,
a curse
can be countered
with a spell of my own.

Then I'll tell my daughters
how I defeated you,
and my sons
how a kind boy
outfoxed you.
I'll be ready.
They'll be ready.

And if you ever
try to find me,
you'll lose again
and again
and again.

We will always
outlive
you.

I trust Wassermann's rage—
we aren't through.
We may never be.

Anyone I ever love
will have to hear
my history
and decide
if I'm too crazy
or dangerous
to love back.

But if love
reduced the monster
to *this*,
his lower lip trembling
as he tries to hold back
a child's tears of frustration,
I have to believe
it will be strong enough again.

Chapter Fifty

There's no right song to accompany
my goodbye to Prague
or the cemetery.

If I ever come back,
it won't be the same.
I'll follow my memories
through the winding streets
instead of a ghost
with forget-me-not eyes.
And any boy
I might fall in love with here
will be just as alive
as I am.

I try to let my hands
and my heart
memorize the letters
on every *matzevah*,
knowing
I can't fit them all
inside of me.

I hold the name of Benjamin's sister
close to me.

Is Helena still alive,
an old woman
somewhere in America,
with stories
lodged in her bones?
Does she still miss her brother—
long gone
       (to her)
but never forgotten?
With enough research, I know
I can find her
or her descendants.

I want to tell them
Benjamin's headstone is still cared for.
I want to tell them
someone still remembers him
and always will.

I still don't know
what it means to be
a chapter in my family's history
or even
to be me.

Does it mean
saying the Shema,
waiting out a flood,
sending a raven
and a dove
into a rain-soaked sky?

Does it mean
moving across borders
like water
moves across stones?

Or does it mean knowing
the Wassermanns of the world
are always one step
behind you?

Maybe
it's all of those things.
Maybe
it's how I choose to live now,
honestly
and with courage.

There is another world waiting
around the corner
for Benjamin and me,
one I'll only see
when my breath
gives out
and flowers grow
from what's left of me.

But I'm not there yet.
Which just means
I'll have to do
enough living
for the both of us.

THE END

Acknowledgments

I am indebted to my agent and friend, Rena Rossner, for her patience, dedication, and belief in my work; my editor, Ashley Hearn, for understanding the heart of Ilana and Benjamin's story so perfectly; and the hardworking team at Peachtree.

This book wouldn't have been possible without the friendship, enthusiasm, and feedback of Roselle Lim, Jessica Russak-Hoffman, Li Wren, Suri Parmar, Josh Gauthier, Paul Bustamante, Dr. Theodora Goss, Jim Kelly, Kip Wilson, Hayley Chewins, Aden Polydoros, Heather Kassner, Celyta Jackson, my father, and my sister, Autumn. I am especially grateful to J.R. Dawson for encouraging me to write this story, Celeste Loring for helping me open the right doors, and my mother for reading every version.

I would like to thank Dr. Steven Reece, Przemek Panasiuk, Rachel McRae, Jo Siegienski, Cindy Jones, Elaine Brown, Marla and Jay Osborn, Vasyl Yuzyshyn,

Bruce Mussey, Dr. Caroline Sturdy Colls, Dan Oren, Avraham Groll, Alon Goldman, Yolanda Czyzewski-Bragues, and the 2019 Jewish Gen scholars for the work they do to remember and honor the dead.

About the Author

R. M. Romero is a Jewish Latina and author of fairy tales for children and adults. She lives in Miami Beach with her cat, Henry VIII, and spends her summers helping to maintain Jewish cemeteries in Poland. You can visit her online at *www.rmromero.com*.